THE DEVIL'S DOZEN

In the underworld of London, the 'Stranger' controlled the 'Devil's Dozen', a gang noted for the daring and murderous nature of their crimes. However, the Stranger intended to betray his gang members to the police and leave himself with all the proceeds of their crimes. Then one gang member found out the Stranger's plan and his identity — and was quickly silenced. Private investigator Philip Quest was determined to unmask the Stranger. Would he live long enough to do it?

Books by Nigel Vane
in the Linford Mystery Library:

THE VEILS OF DEATH
THE MENACE OF LI-SIN
THE MIDNIGHT MEN
THE VANISHING DEATH

NIGEL VANE

THE DEVIL'S DOZEN

Complete and Unabridged

LINFORD
Leicester

First published in Great Britain

First Linford Edition
published 2011

British Library CIP Data

Vane, Nigel.
    The devil's dozen. - -
(Linford mystery library)
1. Gangsters- -England- -London- -Fiction.
2. Private investigators- -England- -
London- -Fiction. 3. Detective and mystery
stories. 4. Large type books.
I. Title II. Series
823.9'12–dc22

ISBN 978–1–4448–0802–5

Published by
F. A. Thorpe (Publishing)
Anstey, Leicestershire

Set by Words & Graphics Ltd.
Anstey, Leicestershire
Printed and bound in Great Britain by
T. J. International Ltd., Padstow, Cornwall

This book is printed on acid-free paper

1

The Stranger

The man seated at the broken, rickety table passed a trembling hand across his forehead, and when he withdrew it the fingers came away damp.

Yet it was not a warm night, cold in fact, and outside raining heavily, as the sound of the drops falling on the grimy skylight that provided both light and ventilation to the disreputable apartment testified.

The room in which he sat was bare and miserable, the floor carpetless and in many cases broken away. In some places an attempt had been made to repair the rotting boards by nailing strips of wood, obviously obtained from some broken boxes that filled one corner, over the holes.

From the damp walls the paper hung in ribbon-like strips, revealing the dirty plaster behind, and in many places this too had fallen away, leaving the bare laths that supported it exposed.

The dim light of a single candle that flared and guttered in the draught from the broken skylight was the only illumination the garret boasted and this sent strange and fitful shadows, grotesque in their ever-changing shapes, dancing a weird and spectral ballet upon the walls and dirty ceiling.

Beyond the table and the chair on which the man sat there was little other furniture in the room. At one side, against the wall behind the door was a tumbled down camp bed, on which lay a heap of disordered rags, which evidently did duty for bedclothes, for they had been thrown back and still remained in the same position as when this owner had last used them. In another corner was a tin basin and a jug, the basin still half full of dirty water, this, together with a battered trunk, almost hidden beneath innumerable labels, long since obliterated, completed the contents of the miserable apartment.

The occupant of the garret was a man whose age it was difficult at first glance to judge. He was thin, almost to the point of emaciation, and his dark hair, plentifully splashed with white, fell in lank strands over his forehead. His face was a greyish white, a peculiar colour, unwholesome and almost dead looking, out of which the dark, lustreless eyes, sunk in deep caverns under which the skin hung loosely in leaden-hued pouches, gazed dreamily into vacancy. The pupils had a trick of alternately contracting and expanding, now large, now so small as to be almost invisible.

His hands were so slender that they seemed almost transparent, scarcely more than skin and bone, and had a habit of playing nervously with any small object that happened to be within reach of the long, sensitive fingers.

And yet Robert Deering was but twenty-five, although he looked old enough for a man of forty or more. Had there been a doctor present the tell-tale eyes of the man at the table would have told their own story, for, written on the face as clearly as though the words themselves had been stamped in indelible ink, were the signs of the drug that had caused his downfall, and was daily sapping away his strength and vitality.

As the light of the candle fell on his face it was possible to discern, through the ravages caused by illness and cocaine, the remnants of breeding that still lingered in the finely-shaped nose and mouth, and, in spite of the weakness of the chin, lent a certain air of distinction to the whole face.

For Robert Deering had not always lived in a garret. There had been times, times which occasionally thrust their way unbidden through his drug-bemused brain, when he had taken his place among the class into which by birth it was his right to belong. He was a university man, and but for a fatal mistake, a youthful escapade which had caused him to be 'sent down,' might well have made his mark in the world in the profession he had chosen.

The episode had led to a violent quarrel with his father, a man, who, though strictly just in all his dealings, was stern and unforgiving towards anyone who lapsed from following the strict principles which he considered right and honourable.

But his son was just as wilful and headstrong as he, and after that final interview had shaken the dust from his feet and left his father's home for ever. He had got in with the wrong set and had slowly sunk lower and lower. Cocaine at last got him in its deadly grip and from drugs to crime was but a short step.

He had received one day a letter typewritten on cheap paper and containing neither date nor address. It merely stated that if he would meet the writer at nine o'clock on the following night in the outer circle of Regent's Park he would hear of something that would be of considerable advantage to himself. It was signed the 'Stranger.'

Deering had heard many references concerning the mysterious sender of the letter from his friends in the underworld of London and knew that the signature concealed the identity of a keen and clever brain, a criminal genius, the mention of whose name caused lesser crooks to speak in hushed voices of his exploits. He also knew that the 'Stranger' controlled a gang known as the 'Devil's Dozen,' a name which it had earned through its absolute unscrupulousness, and the belief that its membership was confined to twelve, though the identity of the actual members of the organisation was unknown.

Deering kept the appointment. The dark stretch of the outer circle was deserted, but punctually at nine o'clock a car appeared and noiselessly drew up beside where he was pacing slowly up and down.

The driver, a muffled figure in a huge coat, for the night was cold and raw, got out and approached him. Deering saw that the man's face was hidden behind the mica goggles he wore.

'I thought you'd come,' said the stranger, and taking Deering by the arm led him over to the side of the car, and there made his proposal, that Deering should become a member of the 'Devil's Dozen.'

Deering, down and out and hungry, needed little persuasion, though many times afterwards he had regretted the step he had taken.

His meeting with the mysterious and unknown leader of the gang had been frequent after that, though never once had he managed to get a glimpse of his face.

His work for the 'Devil's Dozen' had not been an active one. It had been his job to help plan the coups that had baffled the police, but even in this the 'Stranger's' organisation had been so perfected that except on one occasion Deering had never discovered the identity of the other members who constituted the gang.

Presently he closed the book he had been attempting to read, a well used copy of Emerson, and rising unsteadily to his feet started to pace slowly up and down the floor, his hands behind him, his chin sunk low upon his breast, the picture of utter dejection. Money of late had been scarce, and his supply of the drug that gave him for the time being life and vitality, had become exhausted.

Deering was well aware, from experience, of the hours of agony to which his nerves, deprived of the solace, would subject him. Already the terrible reaction which invariably follows the use of the deadly drug had got him in its grip.

Suddenly, in the midst of his pacing, he stopped with a quick gasp, his hand pressed tightly to his side. A sharp spasm of pain had shot through his heart, a pain like the searing of a red hot blade, and he had to clutch at the side of the rickety table to steady himself, while his breath hissed through his teeth in short, irregular pants.

It was not the first time that his overstrained heart had given him a warning. A dose of cocaine would have relieved him instantly, but he knew that there would come a time when even the drug would be useless against those attacks which of late were becoming more and more frequent and of longer duration.

After a short interval he recovered himself a little, but the attack left him weak and trembling, and still holding to the table he lowered himself into the chair.

With a shaking hand he felt in his pocket and found a packet of cheap cigarettes. There was but one, which he lit in the flame of the candle, inhaling the smoke deeply. Under its soothing influence he began presently to feel better. He was still very weak, and his legs when he tried to stand were so shaky that he had to sink back into the chair again.

The first sound of a soft footstep on the stairs outside caused him to raise his head and listen. The footsteps came along the passage and drew nearer and nearer, and finally stopped outside his door. The handle turned gently, and with a creak of the rusty hinges the door opened and a man slipped into the room.

He was of medium height and broad shouldered, and under the dark overcoat that he wore could be glimpsed the black of conventional evening dress. The upper part of his face was concealed behind a black silk mask so that only the bearded chin and firm set mouth were visible.

The visitor closed the door behind him and stood for some moments surveying the occupant of the garret in silence.

'Well,' he said presently, in a low voice, advancing towards the table, 'I suppose you didn't expect a visit from me unless you can guess what I've come about?'

'If you've got some fresh stuff for me to work on,' replied Deering, 'you'll have to let me have some money first. My nerves have gone to shreds and I'm no use to anybody until I can get some more 'snow.''

The masked man laughed, and it was not a pleasant sound, for there was not a vestige of mirth in its tone.

'You're a fool,' he said harshly. 'A fool to yourself. Why don't you cut this drug business out?'

Deering shrugged his thin shoulders.

'What's the use of talking nonsense,' he answered irritably. 'You know very well it's too late now. If I stopped it would kill me.'

'It will kill you anyway,' said the other.

'But I haven't come here to give you lectures for the good of your health. Lately there's been a lot of information leaking out to the police. Somebody's been squealing and I want to find out who it is.'

'Why come to me?' asked Deering.

The Stranger rested a gloved hand on the edge of the table and leaned slightly forward.

'I'll tell you,' he replied. 'The last little coup I planned — or rather we planned together — was frustrated at the last moment by someone who had sent a warning to Scotland Yard.' He paused.

'Go on,' said Deering.

'The only person besides myself,' continued the Stranger emphasising every word, 'who was aware of the particulars and who could have sent the warning — was you!'

He hissed the last words almost in the other's face.

Deering started to his feet, clutching the back of the chair to steady himself.

'Are you accusing me?' he demanded hotly.

The other nodded.

'I am,' he answered shortly.

'Well, you're a liar!' cried Deering, angrily, and into his pale face crept a spot of colour. 'I haven't sunk low enough yet to become a 'nark.' Besides, what object should I have?'

'Of course, you've forgotten that there's a large reward offered,' sneered the man in the mask, 'for any information that will lead to the capture of the 'Devil's Dozen,' and particularly the leader of the gang!'

'Do you suppose I'm after the reward?'

'I think it's quite possible,' retorted the Stranger coolly. 'Anyway, you were the only person who knew anything about the plan for securing the Bridgeport diamonds, so it's fairly obvious who tipped off the police.'

'I've told you I know nothing about it,' said Deering. 'I've held no communication with the police at all. I'm not so fond of them as all that. If I had wanted to give 'em any information and get the reward, as you imagine, I could have told them something really big; something they have been striving to learn for the last eight months.'

He looked straight at the man opposite him.

'What's that?' asked his visitor quickly.

'The real identity of the 'Stranger',' said Deering quietly, watching the effect his words had on the other.

The hand that still rested on the edge of the table clenched itself, and the firm line of the mouth became for a second even more compressed.

'So you know,' was all he said softly.

'Yes, and I've known for some time,' said Deering. 'You're not quite so clever as you imagine, Mr. —'

The Stranger stopped him.

'You are very foolish to have told me,' he broke in, 'for the man who knows me is as good as already dead!'

The words were quietly uttered, icy in their coolness, but that very fact only made them the more menacing.

They did not appear to affect Deering with any uneasiness, however, for he only laughed softly.

'You don't suppose,' he replied, 'that I

should have told you if I hadn't taken precautions beforehand to ensure my personal safety. If you killed me now it wouldn't keep the secret.'

The Stranger regarded him in silence, his eyes gleaming through the holes in the silken mask.

'What exactly do you mean,' he demanded at length.

'I have set down in writing all the knowledge I have acquired concerning you,' replied Deering, 'and the statement has been sent to a safe hiding place, and if anything happens to me it will be opened. It would make interesting reading, I assure you!'

'You're clever,' said the Stranger, his voice vibrating with the rage he was suppressing by sheer force of will, 'very clever. You possess more intelligence than I gave you credit for. May I ask what use you propose to make of your knowledge?'

'None!' said Deering quietly. 'So long as you play the game with me and the rest of the gang. I have only told you part of my discoveries. Now I'll tell you some more.'

The red had faded from his cheeks, leaving them whiter than before. Excitement was, for the moment, lending him false strength.

'You accused me just now,' he continued, 'of squealing to the police. I'm glad you did, for it has given me an opportunity of saying something to you which I've wanted to say for weeks.' He paused and passed the tip of his tongue over his dry lips. 'For a long time now you have been busily engaged in converting all the profits accruing from the atrocities of the 'Devil's Dozen' into cash — notes of high denomination — and you have packed these in half a dozen different boxes which you have deposited at various solicitors' and bankers' in different names. That surprised you, didn't it? You didn't know I knew that?'

'Go on,' said the Stranger shortly.

'For the past four months,' Deering went on, his voice rising as he continued, 'you've been making several excuses for not keeping to your original plans and sharing out every three months, among them being that you have not been able to negotiate the sale of the stuff. This was a lie!'

'You're talking a lot of nonsense,' broke in the Stranger harshly.

'I'm doing nothing of the kind and you know it,' retorted Deering. 'I'm speaking the truth and I don't intend to keep silent and let you double-cross the others.'

'There is no question of double-crossing,' said the other thickly. 'What I have said has been simply the truth. I have not been able to convert the results of the last four jobs into cash and I don't intend to until I can get the price I want.'

'You sold Lady Waring's emerald necklace to old Rosenthal for twenty thousand pounds last month,' said Deering, and checked the items on his fingers as he proceeded. 'The Manton diamonds you got rid of three weeks ago through Morley to an American collector with more dollars than morals, for over a hundred thousand. These are only two cases, and not one penny of the money has been distributed among your associates who did the work and took all the risks.'

'You're wasting your talent,' sneered the Stranger. 'You ought to be at Scotland Yard, Deering, you'd have made a fine detective. It must have taken you a long time to find all this out.'

'It did,' replied Deering. 'I've been suspicious of you for a long time.'

'I don't know where you got your information,' said the other, 'but it's all false. If I had disposed of the stuff and got the money I should have divided it up at once.'

'You wouldn't,' answered Deering. 'You're planning to keep the lot for yourself. You want to know who sent the warning to the police over the Bridgeport affair? I'll tell you — You did!'

'You're mad,' snarled the Stranger. 'Too much drugging has affected your brain.'

'You knew,' continued Deering, taking no notice of the other's interruption, 'that for the first time I was going to take an active part in the affair. You hoped that I should be caught red-handed. That would have got rid of me and only left ten others to deal with. Your idea was to 'shop' each member of the gang as quickly as possible, and as they none of them knew your identity you were safe enough and could clear off with all the proceeds. It was a good idea, but it isn't coming off!'

The Stranger succeeded in mastering the rage which consumed him by a supreme effort.

'Look here, Deering, what's the use of us quarrelling. Suppose we talk the matter over quietly. There is enough and to spare for both of us and I'm willing to divide up with you — on certain conditions,' he added.

Deering leaned across the table.

'So you admit trying to secure the lot for yourself?' he said.

The masked man shrugged his shoulders.

'You appear to know so much,' he retorted, 'that it's not much use my denying it. But I'm willing, as I say, to split it up with you — provided that you destroy that document.'

'What about the rest of the gang?' asked Deering.

The other made an expressive gesture with his hands.

'Why worry about them,' he said. 'After all — '

'You cur!' burst out Deering. 'Do you suppose I'm going to become a party to your double-crossing schemes. I may be pretty much of a rotter, but I'm not quite as bad as all that. You'll either deal fairly by all of us or I shall let Scotland Yard have the information concerning your real identity.'

'You don't suppose for a moment they would believe any charges you made against me, do you?' sneered the Stranger. 'You've got no definite proof and I should deny it. I'm in a position to deny it and they'd certainly believe my word against yours.'

'That's where you're wrong,' replied Deering. 'I've got all the proof needed to convince them anyhow.'

'Where is it?' asked the other sharply.

'Where you can't get it,' retorted Deering.

The Stranger's rage suddenly got the better of him and stretching his long arm across the table he caught Deering by the shoulder and swung him round, the other hand seeking his throat.

'You'll tell me,' hissed the man through his clenched teeth, 'or by Heaven I'll choke the life out of you!'

Deering tried vainly to wrench himself free.

'Let me go,' he panted. 'Am I likely to tell you seeing that that statement is the only safeguard I've got.'

'Where is it?' snarled the Stranger, shaking the thin body of the other. 'Where is it?'

'I tell you — ' began Deering, and broke off sharply.

Again that sharp spasm of pain had shot through him. His face went livid and he strove vainly to get his breath. There came a little gurgling sound in his throat, and with an exclamation of alarm the Stranger felt him go suddenly limp in his arms. Quickly he lowered the inert body to the floor, and stooping, tore open the ragged shirt and laid his hand upon the heart. It had ceased to beat, and the sightless eyes staring upwards at the dirty ceiling were rapidly becoming glazed.

Robert Deering was dead!

His constitution, undermined by drugs, had given way under the unaccustomed strain of the interview.

The Stranger straightened up, thinking quickly.

With Deering's death the danger to himself had assumed a real and alarming aspect, for if the dead man had been speaking the truth, and he had little doubt of the fact, there existed somewhere a document which endangered not only his liberty but even his life. For it was a hanging matter for the Stranger if he were ever caught.

While Deering lived it was bad enough, but there was always the chance of persuading him to destroy the statement or discovering where it was, but now the man was dead the existence of that statement would remain a constant source of dread to the man whose identity it revealed — if it should be opened before he could get it. The thought sent a cold shiver down his spine.

By hook or by crook he must discover

where it had been hidden and destroy it. There was the first possibility that it might be concealed somewhere in the attic.

He searched every likely hiding place but without result. Time was getting on and at any moment someone might come up from the house below, and he had no desire to be found there, particularly with the body of his erstwhile confederate lying dead on the floor.

With a final look round he slipped to the door. He paused with it half open in his hand, listening intently to assure himself that all was quiet downstairs, then he closed the door noiselessly behind him.

On the dark landing outside he stopped and removed the black silk mask and slipped it into his pocket. Then making his way quickly down the dilapidated staircase to the front door, passed out into the street. No one had seen him enter and no one saw him leave. The rain was still falling and the little road was deserted.

Turning up the collar of his coat and

pulling his soft hat down over his eyes the Stranger set off briskly towards Kennington Road which ran across the top at right angles.

He paused for a moment in a dark doorway as he reached the end and his hands went up to his face.

Almost opposite Lambeth North Station a closed car was drawn up to the kerb. With a word to the chauffeur the Stranger stepped in. As the car moved off and he sank back on to the cushions it could have been noticed that whereas the man who had left the Lambeth attic had been bearded, the man who was now being driven swiftly Westwards was clean shaven and possessed a chin as smooth and hairless as a woman's.

2

Philip Quest's Resolve

The Old Bailey was crowded.

Long before the building had been open, its precints had been besieged by people anxious to secure the few remaining seats available to the public.

By nine o'clock it had been necessary to summon a special force of police to clear a path for the ever increasing stream of motor cars and taxi cabs that were constantly arriving, unloading their contents to swell the already overcrowded queue of sightseers.

Most of the crowd had come out of morbid curiosity, for a murder trial always has the effect of drawing like a magnet those people who seem to find their sole enjoyment from the sordid side of life, and take a perverted delight in anything that promises a fresh sensation.

The trial of Jefferson Harlowe had

caused a sensation throughout the country, and now on the last day the sole topic of conversation was centred upon the verdict. Not that there was much doubt about the matter. The newspapers had given full prominence to the affair and to the brilliant defence put up by Norman Carfax, the accused man's counsel. But, in spite of Carfax's efforts, the verdict was almost a forgone conclusion. The evidence had been overwhelmingly against Harlowe from the start.

Harlowe was accused of the murder of Charles Benson, a wealthy city broker, and the theft of a large sum of money — over forty thousand pounds.

Benson had drawn this sum in notes just before the bank had closed on the same day that he met his death, apparently with the intention of completing a business deal early on the following morning. He had returned to his office at four o'clock and his secretary, Jack Archer, had seen him lock the money in the safe. Just as he was leaving Benson had mentioned the fact that he intended working late.

At eight o'clock Beal, the liftman, who usually locked up the offices at that hour, had seen a light under the door of Benson's suite. He had knocked and Benson had answered the summons, saying that he was working late. As all the people who rented offices in the building had keys to the front door, Beal had gone home at ten o'clock, and here was the curious incident that was made much of by the papers: Scotland Yard received a telephone message telling them to send round at once to Benson's offices as a murder had just been committed. The Yard informed the city police and an inspector and a sergeant went round at once.

The main door to the building was unlocked and they had no difficulty in getting in. Benson's offices were on the second floor. Here, too, the door was unlocked and partly open. The outer office was in darkness, but from the inner office came a gleam of light under the communicating door which was closed.

Inspector Mallard on entering this inner office, for the door although shut was not locked, discovered Harlowe standing beside the body of Charles Benson who was lying on the floor close to the big desk which stood in the centre of the room.

He had been stabbed, and the knife with which the crime had been committed still protruded from between his shoulder blades. A large safe that occupied a position behind the door was wide open and the key, attached to a bunch, still dangled in the lock.

Harlowe seemed dazed when arrested, but repeatedly affirmed his innocence and swore that Benson was already dead and the safe opened when he arrived, which was ten minutes before the police.

Of the forty thousand pounds there was not a trace. Jack Archer, however, had seen it locked in the safe, and Beal, the liftman, swore that Benson had not left the office from the time Archer left at five-thirty till the time he, Beal, left at a little after eight-fifteen. It was unlikely that Benson had gone out after that time, taken the money with him, left it somewhere, and returned to the office.

He had not been to his home, which was at Hampstead, and there was nowhere else he could have left the money at that hour of the night.

But neither was it in the possession of Jefferson Harlowe, and this point Norman Carfax had seized upon as one of his chief arguments for the defence.

The window in Benson's private office opened into a narrow side street, and was open when Inspector Mallard had discovered the crime, and the police brought forward a witness, a bank clerk returning late from his work, who had seen a package thrown from a window and picked up by a man waiting below. He could not be certain of the time or the exact window, but thought it was about nine-forty-five.

This certainly accounted for the money not being found on Harlowe, and the police were of the opinion that he had worked with an accomplice.

This Harlowe strenuously denied, and stuck to his story that the crime had been committed before he arrived at the office. He admitted, however, that he had gone with the intention of stealing the forty thousand pounds, and made a statement which had the effect of turning the affair at once into the leading topic of the day.

He stated that he was a member of the notorious 'Devil's Dozen' and in going to rob Benson's office, he was acting on instructions received from the mysterious leader of the gang — the 'Stranger.'

The instructions had arrived on the morning of the crime, by post, and had been accompanied by two keys, one of which opened the main door of the building and the other the outer door of Benson's office. But Harlowe couldn't produce either the letter or the envelope; he said he had burned them.

So much had come out already, during the preceding days of the long trial.

On the morning of what was believed to be the last day and to witness the end of the proceedings, a large grey car slowly nosed its way among the crowd of vehicles and pedestrians and drew to a halt outside the main entrance of the Old Bailey.

A tall, lean man with sharp, clear-cut

features descended from the driving seat and gently pushed his way through the crowds towards the door, followed by a younger man. Among the few people who had not come in order to enjoy merely a morbid sensation were Philip Quest, the well known private detective and his partner, Richard Lester.

Quest was particularly interested in the case, for the 'Devil's Dozen' was a gang which for months the detective had been trying to run to earth, particularly the mysterious and illusive personality that hid its identity under the soubriquet of the 'Stranger.'

Quest had been present throughout the trial of Jefferson Harlowe and had listened carefully to the evidence against the accused man, and, with the aid of Carfax, who Quest knew fairly well, had even managed to secure a private interview with Harlowe.

The result had done nothing to clear up the mystery of Benson's death, but it had convinced Philip Quest of one fact. He felt that Harlowe in this particular case was speaking the truth when he affirmed his innocence.

The detective's long and varied experience had enabled him to sum up a man fairly quickly on sight, and it was seldom that he was wrong in his judgment, and in spite of the fact that he knew Jefferson Harlowe to be a member of the worst criminal organisation that had menaced London for some time, there was something about the man that Quest liked.

But although he had strained every nerve to try and discover some means of proving Harlowe's innocence, he had been unsuccessful, and Quest's own private opinion was, of course, worthless without tangible facts to back it up.

Inspector Mallard, a rather melancholy-looking man, was standing just inside the doorway as Quest and Lester entered, and as he caught sight of them he came forward and shook hands. Mallard was as convinced of Harlowe's guilt as Quest was of the man's innocence, and no amount of argument on the part of the detective could shake this conviction.

'Good morning, Mr. Quest,' greeted

the inspector with the nearest approach to a smile that had ever been seen on his sad looking face. 'You're a bit early. Don't intend missing any of the final scenes, eh?'

Quest laughed.

'I very much doubt whether the final scenes will finish with the verdict, Inspector,' he remarked. 'You imagine that it is quite a simple case, whereas I am equally certain that it is nothing of the sort.'

'You're still convinced that Harlowe is innocent?' asked Mallard.

'I am,' replied Quest. 'For one thing, how do you account for the telephone message received by Scotland Yard warning them of the crime? In my opinion there hasn't been enough attention given to that.'

'It was probably some enemy of Harlowe's,' responded Mallard, 'who knew that he was contemplating the job at Benson's office and gave him away out of spite. Anyhow, that is our theory.'

Quest shook his head.

'I think you are wrong,' he said. 'To me

that episode seems full of significance, and suggests at least a possible solution that also coincides with Harlowe's own story.'

'What is that?' asked the inspector.

'That the whole thing was a carefully prepared 'frame up',' answered Quest quietly.

Mallard pursed his lips sceptically.

'I'm afraid you're allowing your imagination to run away with you, Mr. Quest,' he said.

'Well, well,' answered the detective. 'We shall see.'

This conversation was interrupted by the appearance of Norman Carfax, the counsel for the defence.

He was a tall man, clean shaven with handsome features, after the Greek style. His blue eyes, usually possessing a merry twinkle in their depths, were grave and sombre and his forehead was puckered into a thoughtful frown. He had already donned his wig and gown and nodded to Quest as he approached.

The detective took him on one side out of earshot of the inspector.

'What do you think the verdict will be?' he asked in a low voice.

'There is not a doubt,' answered Carfax gravely. 'I've done my best, but I'm afraid the jury will find him guilty.'

Philip Quest nodded thoughtfully.

'That's my opinion,' he said. 'But I tell you one thing, Carfax, if Jeff Harlowe is found guilty it's going to be the greatest miscarriage of justice that has occurred for years.'

They passed into the dark hall. Policemen in uniform and unmistakable detectives stood about the various entries, and little knots of people, evil-looking and unclean for the most part, lurked in the background or sat on benches and diffused through the stale, musty air that indescribable odour that clings to police vans and prison reception rooms. They were mostly small cases awaiting a hearing in one of the lesser courts.

Philip Quest and Lester accompanied Carfax up the staircase to a black door on which was painted the inscription, 'Counsel and Clerks.'

Carfax held the door open and they

passed through into the court.

The walls were distempered a greenish-grey; the floor was of bare planking, and the only suggestion of dignity was that offered by the canopy over the judge's seat — lined with scarlet baize and surmounted by the Royal Arms.

Carfax led the way into the well of the court and Quest and his partner took their seats on one side of the benches reserved for the counsel.

On the front bench next to the central table, a barrister — the counsel for the prosecution — was already in his place and absorbed in a pile of papers that lay on the desk before him.

Having seen them to their seats Carfax muttered a word of excuse and hurried away.

Lester surveyed with disgust the cheerless room.

'I wonder,' he whispered to Quest, 'why courts are always so sordid and dirty looking.'

'The uncleanness of the criminal,' answered the detective, 'is not only confined to his moral being. Where ever he goes he leaves a trail of actual physical dirt.'

There came the sudden clatter of feet on the gallery stairs and the court began to fill with spectators.

Several junior counsel filed into their seats behind Quest and Lester; the ushers took their stand below the jury box, and inspectors and detectives and miscellaneous officers began to gather in the entries or peer into the court through the small glazed openings in the doors.

The hum of conversation that had been gradually increasing as the court filled suddenly ceased. A door at the back of the däis was flung open; counsel and spectators rose to their feet, and the Judge entered.

As he took his seat all eyes were turned towards the dock. A few minutes later Jefferson Harlowe appeared in company with a warder and stood calmly surveying the court.

He was a tall, broad shouldered, military looking man, his hair and close-cropped moustache an iron grey. He had come through the War with honours and his record in the army had been a good one. The jury filed into their box and the proceedings commenced.

Sir Edward Quilter, the counsel for the prosecution, rose to his feet and continued his examination of a witness where he had left off when the court adjourned on the previous afternoon.

The witness, a small, sandy-haired man, appeared to be in the last stages of nervousness. He was the bank clerk who had been passing at the back of Benson's offices on the night of the murder and had seen the packet thrown from the window.

'You were saying,' began Sir Edward, 'when the court adjourned yesterday, that you were not certain of the exact time when you saw this packet thrown out of a window. Can you give us any idea of the approximate time?'

The little man hesitated.

'I heard a clock strike about ten minutes earlier, sir,' he answered. 'That would be half past nine.'

'Then the time would be, roughly, between nine-thirty and nine-forty-five when the packet was thrown out?' questioned Sir Edward with a glance at the jury,

'Yes, about that,' answered the witness.

'Are you able to describe the man who picked it up?'

'No, sir.'

'But he appeared to have been waiting to receive the packet?'

'Yes. When I first saw him he was standing at the edge of the pavement looking upwards. I wondered what he was doing. Then I saw something white, that looked like an envelope, fall at his feet. He picked it up and ran and I lost sight of him down a side street.'

Sir Edward sat down.

'Do you propose to cross-examine the witness?' enquired the Judge, seeing that Carfax made no sign.

'No, my Lord,' he replied.

The Judge looked at Sir Edward.

'Are you calling any more witnesses?' he asked, dipping his pen in the ink.

'No, my Lord,' replied Sir Edward. 'That is our case.'

Carfax rose.

'I call one witness, my Lord — the prisoner, whom I shall put in the box in order that he may make a statement on oath.'

Harlowe was then conducted from the dock to the witness-box and was duly sworn. A brief cross-examination followed. He could bring no evidence to account for his movements on the night of the crime, and a point that might have held in his favour, the time at which he had arrived at Benson's office, was impossible to prove. Harlowe repeated the statement he had stuck to throughout the trial, that Benson had been dead when he arrived and the safe already open. Sir Edward tried to shake his story, but failed, and finally sat down. The prisoner was led back to the dock and the court settled itself to listen to the speeches of the counsel.

'My Lord and gentlemen of the jury,' began Carfax, in his clear mellow voice, 'I do not propose to occupy your time with a long speech.'

He touched lightly on the evidence incriminating Harlowe, lingering on the small amount in his favour and stressing the fact of the telephone message to Scotland Yard.

It was a brilliant speech and had he possessed the slightest material to work on there is not a doubt that it would have secured a verdict in the accused man's favour. But even a King's Counsel cannot supply facts that are not there.

Philip Quest, his keen grey eyes watching the jury, knew that in the face of the evidence for the prosecution, it had failed to impress them.

There was a little murmur of applause from the spectators as Carfax sat down, instantly suppressed by the Judge as Sir Edward Quilter rose to make his reply.

His speech was shorter than Carfax's and point by point he itemised the facts against Harlowe.

As he finished, and sat down, the Judge turned over his notes and prepared to address the jury in a manner at once persuasive and confidential. His summing up was perfectly fair and impartial, but as he continued, every word that fell from his lips only served to impress more fully the fact of Harlowe's guilt.

At the end of the Judge's speech the jury left the box and slowly filed out; the Judge retired through the door at the back of his seat, and a little buzz of conversation broke out.

In the part reserved for the Press the reporters' pens were racing over the copy papers, getting ready for the early editions.

Lester allowed his eyes to travel round the crowded court and presently they rested on the figure of a girl. She was sitting near the front and was well but quietly dressed in black, her hands clasped in her lap and her head bent. As he looked she raised it and Lester saw her face. It was deathly pale but so beautiful that Quest's young partner caught his breath and, although he knew that it was anything but good taste, continued to stare at her.

Her face was a perfect oval framed in hair the colour of spun gold, which escaped in little curls from beneath her close-fitting black hat.

Subconsciously she must have become

aware of Lester's stare, for suddenly she turned her head and gazed straight in his direction, while into her pale face crept a tinge of colour as she caught the admiration in his glance. The next instant she had dropped her eyes again and continued to stare at the folded hands in her lap.

Lester nudged Quest's arm.

The detective, who had been sitting lost in thought, turned towards his partner.

'What is it?' he asked.

'I've just seen the most beautiful girl in the world,' whispered Lester. 'Look — near the front in the centre.'

Philip Quest allowed his mouth to relax into a smile. He was used to Lester's impressionable nature. He turned his eyes, however, in the direction indicated, but he never saw the object of his young partner's interest for at that moment the return of the Judge caused the whole court to rise. Almost immediately after the jury returned. When they were all in the box the grey-wigged clerk of the court stood up and addressed them.

'Are you agreed upon your verdict,

gentlemen?' he asked in a sing-song voice.

The foreman rose.

'We are,' he announced.

'Do you find the prisoner guilty or not guilty?'

'Guilty!' replied the foreman, slightly raising his voice.

There was a solemn hush as the words fell from his lips, broken only by the faint sound of a choked back sob from some of the women present.

The Judge, after the usual formalities, affixed the black cap and pronounced the dread sentence — the extreme penalty that the law demands for wilful murder.

In a few moments it was all over and it was with a sigh of relief that Philip Quest found himself outside the stuffy court.

'Well,' said Inspector Mallard, as he caught sight of Quest and his partner, 'that's over!'

'Not quite over,' replied the detective quietly 'You've got the wrong man, Mallard.'

'The jury didn't seem to think so,' replied the inspector.

'The jury,' answered Philip Quest,

'brought in a verdict in accordance with the evidence laid before them. To-day is Wednesday,' he continued irrelevantly, 'according to the law three clear Sundays must elapse between a sentence and the execution. There is not much time.'

He spoke as though voicing his thoughts aloud, and Lester and Inspector Mallard stared at him in astonishment.

'Time for what?' asked the inspector.

'Time to find the man who sent that telephone message to Scotland Yard,' answered Quest grimly. 'The man who planned the 'frame up' against Harlowe; the real murderer of Charles Benson! For if it is humanly possible I'm going to find him and save an innocent man from suffering for a crime he never committed.' And leaving Mallard open-mouthed, the detective passed through the entrance and climbed into his car.

Quest was silent on the way back to the city, and Lester, who knew that his partner was thinking deeply, checked the questions that hovered on the tip of his tongue and left the detective to his reverie.

Quest put the car up and they walked the short distance from the garage to their office. The burly, thick-set figure of Detective-Inspector Johnson was pacing impatiently up and down the consulting-room as they entered.

'Hello, Quest,' he jerked, thrusting out a stubby hand. 'Glad you've come. Wasn't going to wait much longer.'

'What's the trouble, Johnson?' asked Quest.

'Want you to come round with me to Portman Square,' puffed the inspector, red in the face and almost breathless in his efforts to speak quickly enough. 'Sir Lionel Trevor's house was broken into during the night and Sir Lionel murdered, and unless I'm very much mistaken, Quest, the crime is the work of the 'Devil's Dozen'!'

3

The Burned Paper

As the taxi containing Philip Quest, Lester and Detective-Inspector Johnson swung round into Portman Square it was easy for the occupants to distinguish at a glance the house in which the crime had been committed.

A uniformed constable stood on guard at the door, and scattered about the pavement were little knots of loungers gazing interestedly up at the windows, though what they expected to see was a matter known only to themselves.

Johnson had been giving Quest a brief outline of the affair as they drove along.

It was one of the maids who first discovered that there was anything wrong. Sir Lionel Trevor's invariable custom was to have a cup of tea taken to his bedroom at seven-thirty each morning. As usual the servant had knocked, but without being able to get any answer. After trying several times she had opened the door, which was unlocked, and looked in. Sir Lionel was not there. The bed had, however, been slept in, for the clothes were disturbed. Thinking that for some reason her master had risen early, she was not at first alarmed but carried the tea back to the kitchen.

At breakfast time, which was at eight-thirty, there was no sign of Sir Lionel, and Reed, the butler, made a search of the house. The study, which was situated at the back and looked out on to the garden, was locked, and repeated knocking on the door failed to elicit any response. The butler was by now becoming alarmed and decided to go round to the french windows which opened from the study on to a balcony. The breakfast room windows opened the same way and going out by these, Reed had passed along the balcony to the windows of the study. One of them stood ajar and going into the room the butler had made the terrible discovery.

The study was in the utmost confusion,

and lying by the door, clad only in pyjamas and a dressing-gown, was the body of Sir Lionel. He was stone dead and had been shot squarely through the forehead.

Reed had immediately called a policeman, who had communicated with Scotland Yard.

Inspector Johnson had barely time to acquaint Quest with these meagre details before the cab pulled up at the door of the house of death.

'I've arranged for everything to be left untouched until you've had a look round,' said the Inspector, as they got out and ascended the steps, eyed curiously by the waiting sightseers.

An Inspector, whom Johnson had left in charge, was standing in the hall as they entered and came forward saluting.

'I suppose you will wish to see the study first, sir?' he asked as Johnson introduced the detective.

Philip Quest nodded as he laid his hat and gloves on the table in the hall. They followed the man up the stairs to a wide landing on the first floor. From this ran two short corridors to left and right.

The Inspector turned down the passage on the right and stopped before the second door, near the staircase end. Taking a key from his pocket he stooped and unlocked it.

The room they entered was large and comfortably furnished, the predominating colour scheme being blue and biscuit colour.

In the centre stood a large, flat-topped desk of carved oak, its surface being covered with dark blue leather. Several settees and armchairs were scattered about, beside which stood three or four low smoking-tables piled untidily with books and newspapers. One of these had been overturned and lay on its side, the contents scattered over the floor.

The walls were surrounded with low bookcases covered with glass doors. The doors stood open and the books had been pulled out and were lying in an untidy heap on the carpet in front of them.

Every drawer in the desk had been emptied and the papers and other articles they had contained flung carelessly about in all directions. The whole room had been turned upside down and had the appearance of having been struck by a cyclone.

Close by the door, a little to the right, lay the figure of an elderly man, rigid and still, his sightless eyes staring horribly at the ceiling.

Philip Quest paused on the threshold and his keen eyes travelled round the room, lingering for a moment only on each object, taking in, with that marvellous comprehensive and retentive power of observation, for which he was famous, every detail. Finally he allowed his gaze to dwell on the grim thing on the floor.

Quest had his own methods of investigation; methods which those people who were unacquainted with the detective's peculiarities were wont to regard with a half-contemptuous toleration, and who received something of a shock when Quest achieved his amazing results.

Detective-Inspector Johnson, however, had, deep in his heart, a profound admiration for the famous private detective, although it was doubtful if he would admit the fact even to himself, and watched with interest as Quest commenced his investigations.

The detective turned his attention first to the body, and dropping on to one knee beside it studied it with close attention, particularly the face, which was contorted into an expression of the utmost horror and surprise.

He carefully examined the small blue mark in the centre of the forehead from which had trickled a faint thin line of blood. For a second or two he peered at it and then looked up at Johnson.

'I should say the shot was fired from an automatic,' he remarked. 'The wound has the appearance of having been caused by a nickel-jacketed bullet.'

He raised the head slightly. The carpet beneath was soaked with blood, which had come from a larger wound at the back of the skull.

'The murderer must have fired at close range,' he continued. 'There are distinct traces of powder marks on the forehead and the bullet has passed right through the head.'

'It lodged in the wall,' grunted Johnson, jerking his bristly head in the direction of the door. 'I prized it out.'

'I'd like to have a look at it in a moment,' murmured the detective, closely scrutinising the hands of the dead man, which were tightly clenched in his last death agony.

As Quest came to the right hand he bent his head lower, with a little exclamation, and unclosed the index finger. He removed something that was adhering to the nail, and straightened up, holding it between his finger and thumb. It looked like a long black hair.

'What is it?' asked Lester, eagerly bending forward. 'A hair?'

The detective shook his head.

'No,' he answered, transferring the object to the palm of his hand.

Johnson and Quest's partner bent over him and looked at it curiously. It was a thin strand of fine black silk, slightly unravelled at the end, and almost gossamer-like in its texture.

'I wonder how that came to be in his hand,' said Johnson thoughtfully.

'It wasn't in his hand,' replied Quest. 'It was caught in a broken piece of finger nail. I should say that Sir Lionel threw out his hand to ward off his murderer and caught his nail in part of the assassin's attire.'

'Good Heavens, Quest!' ejaculated Johnson, as an idea suddenly struck him. 'Could it possibly have been a woman who killed him?'

'You mean — ' began Quest.

'It's a strand of the thinnest and finest silk,' continued the Inspector excitedly, 'and that kind of material is seldom found in a man's clothes.'

Philip Quest rose slowly to his feet. Suddenly bending his head he sniffed gently at the silken thread.

'There is no trace of perfume,' he remarked. 'But that doesn't tell us much, there are some women who never use it.'

He remained in thoughtful silence for a moment and then:

'What makes you think that this is the work of the 'Devil's Dozen'?' he asked.

'I'll tell you,' said Johnson, and led the

way over to a small table that stood by the french windows.

A sheet of paper had been spread on the top and neatly laid out on this were three small objects. A long lump of irregularly shaped metal; a piece of thin elastic, about two inches long; and a charred and blackened paper.

Detective-Inspector Johnson picked this last carefully up in his stubby fingers, handling it gently.

'I found this in the grate,' he said triumphantly to Quest. 'Look! You can still manage to read one or two words here and there and the signature is quite clear, although the greater part has been destroyed.'

Quest took it and examined it carefully, first with the naked eye and then with the aid of his powerful pocket lens.

The words were disjointed but seemed to have formed part of a letter, and ran:

' . . . Deering . . . sent . . . the box . . . your life . . . unless . . . returned . . .
'THE STRANGER.'

The letter had been typewritten and was plainly visible, for the upper part of the paper had suffered most by the fire.

Quest's eyes gleamed slightly as he gently laid the fragile document back on the table.

'There doesn't seem to be much doubt that the 'Devil's Dozen' were responsible for the crime,' he agreed. 'I suppose this is the bullet?' He indicated the small lump of metal.

Johnson nodded and the detective picked it up in his long, thin fingers.

'It came from an automatic as I thought,' said Quest. 'Of a heavy calibre too, I should imagine.'

He commenced a thorough search of the room, working away from the body and beginning with the window through which the murderer must have gained access to the study. The fastening was a simple one and there were marks which showed plainly where it had been forced. The carpet was cut to fit the room exactly and was of a material that yielded not a trace of footprints.

'I suppose you have questioned the

servants?' said Quest, when he had finished.

'Yes,' answered Johnson, 'but they can give no information that is likely to help us.'

'None of them heard any sound during the night?'

The Scotland Yard man shook his head.

'Humph!' said Quest. 'The murderer must have used a silencer, otherwise they'd have been bound to have heard the shot. An automatic is anything but a noiseless weapon, and in the middle of the night would have been certain to have wakened the house. From the condition of the body I should imagine that Sir Lionel met his death between two-thirty and three this morning.'

'The divisional surgeon said it was round about that time,' said Johnson. 'The most mysterious part of the whole affair is the motive, for as far as I can ascertain, nothing has been stolen.'

Lester looked round the ransacked and disordered apartment.

'Whoever it was who committed the crime,' he remarked, 'it's fairly obvious that he was searching for something concealed in this room. I shouldn't think there is a thing in the place that hasn't been moved.'

'Certainly robbery wasn't the motive,' said Quest meditatively, his eyes straying to a glass case set against the wall which contained a collection of gold and silver ornaments and trinkets. 'No burglar would have missed that.'

'What could he possibly have been after?' asked Johnson, running his fat fingers through his short hair, a favourite trick of his when he was worried or thoughtful.

'The letter mentioned a box. I should say that was what he was after,' replied the detective.

'Do you think the 'Stranger' is the murderer?' asked Lester.

'Either he or one of the gang,' said Quest. 'The crime itself, of course, is easy to reconstruct. Sir Lionel must have been disturbed by some noise which awoke him and he came down to find out the cause. He surprised the searcher, whoever it was, and was shot before he could give the alarm. Of course, there may have been more than one person concerned in the affair, we can't tell yet.'

Quest had crossed to the window while he had been speaking and now he opened it, stepping out on to the stone balcony. It ran the length of the house and was divided in the centre by a flight of steps that led downward to the garden.

It was hopeless to look for any traces on the hard stone, as the detective saw at a glance, but a gravel path ran along at the foot of the steps and Quest made his way down to this, Lester and Johnson remaining on the balcony. He might have saved himself the trouble, however, as he presently found, for the gravel yielded nothing in the nature of a clue.

There had been no rain for some days and the gravel path was almost as hard as the stone above. With a disappointed shrug of the shoulders Quest returned to the study.

'I should like to speak to the butler,' he said, and the Inspector who had led them to the room and had remained a silent spectator during the detective's investigations, hurried away at a word from Johnson in search of Reed, the butler.

'The name in the half-burnt letter,' said Quest musingly, as they waited for the butler to arrive. 'I've heard it before somewhere — Deering — Deering' He passed his hand across his forehead and frowned in an effort to recapture the fugitive memory.

'I know,' broke in Lester, suddenly. 'I remember pasting an account of his death in the 'index' the other day. He was found dead in a garret in Lambeth about three weeks ago!'

'That's right,' said Quest. 'I knew I'd heard the name before. He died from heart disease brought on by cocaine. He was a confirmed drug taker and was known generally as 'Snowy' Deering on that account.'

'I remember him well,' grunted Johnson. 'We suspected him for a long time for being on the crook, but we could never pull anything on him. He's dead, so I don't see how he can be connected with this case,' he added.

'His name's mentioned in that letter from the 'Stranger,'' replied Quest, 'so he must have been associated in some way with the 'Devil's Dozen.''

At that moment there came a tap at the door and Reed entered the room. He kept his eyes averted from the form on the floor and looked from one to the other nervously.

'You wished to speak to me, sir?' he enquired in a low voice, at last letting his eyes rest on Johnson.

He was of medium height, fresh-coloured, with close-cropped hair of a light sandy colour.

'Mr. Quest wishes to speak to you,' said the Inspector.

'I just want to ask you one or two questions,' said the detective quietly. 'Did you hear any sound during the night — anything out of the ordinary?'

'No, sir, I heard nothing at all, but the cook did,' he added.

'Oh, the cook did,' said Quest. 'What did she hear?'

'She sleeps on the floor below the other servants, sir,' said the butler. 'And she says that during the night she heard a thud from somewhere below. She thought it was a door shutting for she says that's what it sounded like, but she didn't hear anything else, so she went to sleep again.'

'Why didn't she tell me that when I questioned her this morning?' growled Johnson with a glare at the man.

'She didn't think of it till after, sir,' replied Reed. 'I suppose she was too agitated.'

The worthy Inspector snorted.

'What time was it when she heard the noise?' asked Quest.

'I don't know, sir,' replied Reed shaking his head. 'I asked her the same question myself, but she didn't know. She said she seemed to have been asleep for a long time.'

'I'll question her myself presently,' said the detective. 'Now, Reed, can you tell us if Sir Lionel has received a parcel or a box lately?'

The butler thought for a moment.

'What sort of parcel, sir?' he asked.

'I'm afraid I can't give you a description of it,' replied Quest. 'But has he received any kind of package either through the post or by hand?'

'There was a box containing some clothes from his tailor,' replied Reed. 'And a parcel of books from the publishers. I can't recollect any other, sir. Perhaps Miss Nesbitt could help you.'

Philip Quest glanced at him quickly.

'Who is Miss Nesbitt?' he asked, sharply.

'She was Sir Lionel's secretary, sir,' answered the butler.

'Where is she now?'

'I don't know,' replied Reed. 'I believe Sir Lionel gave her the day off.'

'Does she live in the house?'

'No, sir. She comes at ten o'clock every morning and leaves at six.'

'You say Sir Lionel gave her the day off. She hasn't been here this morning, then?'

'No, sir.'

'What time did she leave last night?'

'A little earlier than usual, sir — about half-past-five. That's when I heard Sir Lionel tell her she could have to-day off, just as she was leaving.'

'H'm,' said Quest, thoughtfully. 'If she left at five-thirty last night and hasn't been back since she probably knows nothing about this affair yet. Do you know where Miss Nesbitt lives?'

'In Bloomsbury, sir,' answered the butler. 'Just off Russell Square.'

He mentioned an address and Lester noted it down.

'All right, Reed,' said Quest in dismissal, and the man bowed and withdrew.

The detective remained gazing abstractedly at the window for some seconds in silence, then he turned to Detective-Inspector Johnson.

'I don't think there is anything more to be learned here,' he said. 'As soon as possible I'd like to get in touch with Miss Nesbitt. She may be able to tell us something about the box.'

'I suppose you are referring to the box mentioned on that scrap of paper?' said Lester.

'Yes,' replied Quest, walking towards the door.

'You think it was the motive for the crime?' asked Johnson, following and rubbing vigorously at his bristly moustache with a stubby forefinger.

'Not for the murder,' answered the detective, pausing with his hand on the door handle. 'Sir Lionel was killed, I'm convinced, merely because he accidentally interrupted the intruder in his search. It is obvious that something in this house was of vital importance to the 'Devil's Dozen.' Of such vital importance that they were willing to take a considerable risk in order to obtain possession of it. The evidence we obtain from the half-burnt letter indicates that what they were after was a box or something contained in a box. Whether they got it or not we can't say, but I'm inclined to think that they did.'

'Why?' enquired his partner.

'Because they confined their attentions to the study only,' said Quest. 'If the intruder had failed to find what he had been searching for he would have tried some other part of the house.'

'Unless he got scared after the murder and gave it up,' put in Johnson.

Quest shook his head.

'I don't think it is likely,' he replied. 'The place has been thoroughly over-hauled, and it would be a strange coincidence if Sir Lionel had hit upon the exact moment when the marauder had finished his work to interrupt him. Of course it's possible, but quite improbable.'

'That letter looks as if the 'Stranger' had tried to get what he wanted from Sir Lionel by a threat, and failing that, resorted to the robbery as a last resource,' said Lester.

'Why didn't Sir Lionel inform the police directly he received it?' growled Johnson. 'We could have set a trap. It would have been a fine chance to have landed the 'Stranger.' I'd give something to know his true identity, Quest.'

'So would I,' said Quest with a grim smile. 'And so would a good many other people I could mention.' He opened the door and they passed out of the room of death. 'Before we go,' said the detective, as they descended the stairs, 'I think I'll just have a word with the cook about the noise she heard during the night.'

While Quest went off to make his enquiries, Johnson found the Inspector and sent him to make arrangements for the removal of the body, which had been delayed in order that Philip Quest could conduct his investigations.

The detective soon returned.

'There's nothing further to be learnt from the servants,' he announced. 'I shall start my — '

His words were interrupted by a sharp rat-tat on the front door, followed by a prolonged peal of the bell.

Reed appeared apparently from nowhere and crossed the hall to answer the summons and opened the door.

A girl stood on the threshold, and she looked nervous and agitated.

'I've just heard the terrible news,' she said as the butler stood aside, and she stepped into the hall. 'Oh, Reed, is it true about Sir Lionel?' Her voice was husky and scarcely audible.

'Yes, Miss,' answered Reed. 'It's a dreadful affair. How did you know, I thought you were not coming to-day?'

'I saw it in an early edition of the papers,' she said, 'and —'

She broke off as she caught sight of the little group in the hall. Philip Quest stepped forward.

'Miss Nesbitt, I believe,' he said quietly. 'My name is Philip Quest. You were Sir Lionel Trevor's private secretary, were you not?'

The girl looked at him nervously for a moment and then seeming to gain more composure, she answered in a low voice,

'Yes, I am Miss Nesbitt.'

'I was coming round to your private address,' continued Quest, 'in the hope of finding you at home, as I wanted to ask you one or two questions. But now that you are here it will save time if you will answer them now, and time in a case like this is a consideration. Will you come into the dining room, it will be more comfortable there, I think.'

The girl nodded, and Quest led the way into a room on the left. The hall had been dark but as the detective opened the door and held it for the girl to pass through the light from the room beyond fell full upon her and Lester suppressed a gasp of astonishment as he recognised the girl that had attracted his attention at the Old Bailey during the trial of Jefferson

Harlowe that morning. Philip Quest had his back to him and failed to notice his partner's surprised expression, but he had seen something else. Something that caused his lips to compress and his keen eyes to narrow for a second. The girl was dressed entirely in black and wore a coat of fine silk, trimmed with fur at the collar. Near the right shoulder was a small tear that had caused the material to fray slightly, and the threads were of the same hue and texture as the one Quest had removed a short while before from the broken finger nail of the dead man upstairs!

4

A Visit to Lambeth

Was it possible that this girl, who could be little more than twenty-one, was concerned with the killing of Sir Lionel?

Johnson had suggested that the murderer was a woman when Quest had discovered the silken thread adhering to Sir Lionel's finger nail, and yet the detective found it difficult to believe that the girl before him could have had anything to do with the crime.

Certainly no one knew who constituted the membership of the 'Devil's Dozen' and it was possible that this girl was one of their members, but the detective found it hard to believe that this innocent-looking child, for she was little else, with the pale face and the dark-circled blue eyes, could be in any way connected with such an unscrupulous organisation as the 'Devil's Dozen' was known to be.

But Quest was by no means going to overlook the possibility on that account. In the long course of his adventurous career he had come across many criminals of the opposite sex who had, outwardly, appeared just as child-like and innocent as the girl before him. It might prove to be only a coincidence that she was wearing a coat of the same silken material as that of which the thread was composed, but there was the slight ladder-like tear near the shoulder which was precisely the kind of tear that would have been produced by a sharp finger nail catching in the cloth.

These thoughts passed like a flash through Philip Quest's mind, so quickly in fact, that the time they occupied was only the few seconds taken by the girl to cross the room to the big table.

'Sit down, Miss Nesbitt,' said the detective gently, as he followed her into the room and shut the door after Lester and Johnson had entered. 'I shan't keep you very long.'

She seated herself on a chair by the dining-table. She looked uncomfortable and ill at ease and her little gloved hands fidgeted with the clasp of the bag in her lap.

'What is your full name?' began Quest.

'Audrey Nesbitt,' she answered.

'There are one or two points about this case, Miss Nesbitt,' Quest continued, 'in which I think you might be able to help us.'

The girl looked up at him, her large blue eyes wide with astonishment.

'I, Mr. Quest,' she faltered in a voice that held in it a trace of alarm. 'But I know nothing about it except what I've just read in the papers. How can I possibly help you?'

'You held the position of secretary to Sir Lionel,' replied Quest, 'and therefore must have been to a certain extent in his confidence, Miss Nesbitt. How long had you been in his employ?'

The girl thought for a moment before replying.

'Nearly two years, I think,' she answered.

'And I presume as his secretary you knew a fair amount about his private affairs?'

'Only just sufficient to enable me to carry out my duties,' she said. 'Sir Lionel was a very reticent man.'

'But you would naturally deal with his correspondence and open and answer his letters,' said the criminologist.

She nodded.

'Except those that were of a private nature,' she replied. 'He attended to those himself.'

'They would of course be marked 'personal?''

'Some of them. There were others, but I got to know the handwriting.'

'Can you recollect any letter that came by post or by hand recently,' continued Quest, 'that seemed to cause Sir Lionel any uneasiness. Think carefully, Miss Nesbitt, for the matter is important.'

His question evidently startled her, for she looked up quickly and Quest thought he detected a faint trace of fear in her eyes.

'No, Mr. Quest,' she replied after a moment's thought, shaking her head. 'I don't remember Sir Lionel receiving any letter lately that appeared to worry him at all. If there was one, I knew nothing about it.'

'Did Sir Lionel ever mention a gang of criminals called the 'Devil's Dozen?'' Quest shot the question suddenly, his keen eyes fixed on the girl's face.

This time there was no mistaking her agitation. Her face blanched and the colour even receded from her lips, leaving them grey and bloodless, and she raised one hand suddenly to her mouth. For some moments she remained silent and when she did speak her voice was so low that it scarcely rose above a whisper.

'No — no,' she replied. 'That is — only once — in the course of conversation.'

'When was that?' asked the detective, watching her narrowly.

By a visible effort the girl pulled herself together.

'It was one day about three weeks ago, when Mr. Carfax was here. They were discussing some exploit of the 'Devil's Dozen'' — she hesitated slightly, a fact that was not lost on the detective. 'And Sir Lionel remarked that it was time the police did something to put a stop to the menace and that they must be a lot of dunderheads at Scotland Yard.'

Quest repressed a smile as he heard a little wrathful snort from Inspector Johnson.

'And was that the only time that Sir Lionel said anything concerning the gang?' he asked.

'The only time to my knowledge,' Audrey answered.

Quest paused deliberately before he put his next question. He was watching the girl keenly and he was convinced that she knew more about the affair than she wanted them to believe.

'Did Sir Lionel know or ever have any communication with a man called Deering?' he questioned sharply.

She gave a little, half-stifled cry and her hands gripped suddenly and convulsively on the arms of her chair.

'What is the matter, Miss Nesbitt, aren't you feeling well?'

'No, no. I shall be all right in a minute,' she stammered. 'It was just a passing faintness. The shock of this dreadful business has been rather too much for me. I'm very sorry, Mr. Quest, to be so silly.'

Quest knew that she was lying; knew that it was the mention of Deering's name that had affected her so strangely, and waiting till she had had time to recover herself, he repeated the question.

She kept her eyes fixed on her lap as she answered.

'I have never heard the name before,' she murmured, almost inaudibly.

'You are quite sure of that?' persisted Quest.

'Quite,' she whispered huskily.

'Part of a letter has been found in Sir Lionel's study,' continued the detective, 'from which it is obvious that Deering at some time or other sent Sir Lionel a box. Do you know anything about this box?'

She shook her head, her lips were trembling so violently that she was incapable of speech.

Quest felt that it was useless to question her further, although he was certain that she was deliberately withholding knowledge that would have gone a long way towards helping to clear up the mystery.

'There is just one thing more I wish to ask you, Miss Nesbitt,' he said, and his glance was searching. 'Have you ever heard of a mysterious individual called the 'Stranger?''

His question startled her and into her blue eyes there crept an expression of fear.

'I — I — ' Her voice faltered and broke and then suddenly she burst into a paroxysm of tears.

Philip Quest crossed quickly to the girl's side and laid a hand gently on her heaving shoulders.

'Come, come,' he murmured kindly, 'you mustn't cry. I know that this terrible affair has greatly upset you. It is but natural. I won't ask you any more questions now. The best thing you can do will be to go home and rest.'

She stifled her sobs and raised her tear-stained face to Quest.

'You are very kind,' she said simply. 'I think I will take your advice. I don't feel very well.'

With the help of the detective's arm she rose unsteadily to her feet.

'I'll come with you and see you into a taxi,' said Quest.

She thanked him, and her voice was almost steady as she murmured good-bye to Johnson and Lester and went out with Quest.

A taxi was passing and the detective signalled it. As it drew up to the kerb the detective opened the door and assisted the girl inside.

'Here is my card, Miss Nesbitt,' he said as the girl settled herself into the seat. 'If you should remember anything that is likely to be of value in clearing up the mystery surrounding the death of Sir Lionel Trevor,' he said significantly, 'I should be glad if you will communicate with me at that address.'

'I know nothing,' she replied, but her eyes refused to meet his steady gaze. 'Nothing beyond what I have already told you.'

Quest's eyes became grim and stern as he wished her good-bye and closed the door of the cab. He had offered the girl a chance of taking him into her confidence and she had practically turned it down.

The taxi moved off and the detective stood looking after it for some moments, a strange expression on his keen, alert face. Then he turned on his heel and retraced his steps to the dining room.

'I say,' said Lester eagerly as he entered, 'that's the girl I was trying to point out to you in the court this morning.'

'What! Miss Nesbitt?'

'Yes. It's an extraordinary coincidence, isn't it.'

'It's more than a coincidence,' said the detective thoughtfully.

'She knows a great deal more than she admits, Quest,' said Johnson. 'I'm positive she's had something to do with the murder. Why should Deering's name have affected her like it did?'

'I'm perfectly certain that she knows something,' agreed Quest. 'By the way, Johnson, I wish you'd look up Deering's record at the Yard. You've had him under observation for some time. You must have got quite a lot of information about him.'

Johnson nodded his bristly head.

'I will, Quest,' he replied. 'I'm going back to the Yard now and I'll set Records into it right away, and let you have the result at your office.'

'In the meanwhile, Lester,' said the detective, turning to his partner, 'I want you to go to Miss Nesbitt's address at once, keep an eye on the house and note who calls. If the girl goes out, follow her; find out where she goes and who she sees. If she tries to communicate with anybody by letter phone me at once, but in any case report to the office directly you get any results.'

'Right,' said Richard Lester, his eyes sparkling at the prospect of activity.

'You've got the address?' asked Quest and Lester nodded. 'Then off you go.' And Lester departed with a cheery grin at Johnson, on his mission.

'What do you expect to learn by having the girl watched?' asked the Scotland Yard man, when they were alone.

Philip Quest shrugged his shoulders.

'I don't know,' he replied briefly. 'But if the girl has any knowledge of this business, and her behaviour was certainly strange, she'll try and communicate with the 'Stranger' at the first opportunity, and if she does, Lester will follow her. In the meantime the only tangible clue we've got is the letter. Since it refers to Deering, I'm going to make a few enquiries at Lambeth. Do you recollect the address?'

'I can soon get it,' replied Johnson, and made his way to the phone.

He found the dining room deserted on his return, and discovered that Quest had gone back to the study.

When Johnson entered he was engaged in examining the piece of elastic which he had taken from the table on which it had been lying. The body of Sir Lionel Trevor had been removed.

'Deering's address was forty-five Gall Street,' said Johnson. 'It's a little street running off Kennington Road, near Lambeth North Station.'

Quest nodded absently. He was holding the strip of elastic in his hand and turning it this way and that in his long, sensitive fingers.

'What do you make of this, Johnson?'

he said presently.

The burly Inspector crossed to his side and peered at the small object with his protruding eyes. The elastic was grey in colour and in one place spotted with a brownish stain.

'It looks like blood, Quest,' he announced.

'It is blood, Johnson,' said the detective. 'And it suggests rather an interesting possibility.'

'What do you mean?' queried Johnson.

'It provides us with a clue that should make it fairly easy to identify the murderer of Sir Lionel, when we come across him,' replied Philip Quest.

'Or her,' said Johnson, significantly.

'Or her,' agreed the detective. 'Though I'm inclined to think it was a man.'

'Well, whoever it was, how is that stain going to help us?' demanded the puzzled Inspector.

'Think it out, Johnson,' said Quest, with a slight twinkle in his eye. 'Think what the elastic was likely to have been used for and you'll see what I mean.' He put it back on the table and turned to the door. 'I'm going to Lambeth now, if anything fresh occurs, let me know at once.'

The Inspector accompanied him down the stairs as far as the hall and then went in search of the man he was leaving in charge to give him some final instructions, still puzzling over Quest's cryptic words.

Philip Quest left the house and, hailing a taxi, drove to Lambeth North Tube Station.

He experienced no difficulty in finding Gall Street, which was a narrow cul-de-sac, little more than an alley. It was indescribably dirty, and the tumble-down houses which lined each side of the road were almost falling to pieces with age and neglect. The roadway, if it were possible to dignify it by that name, was full of litter and refuse about which groups of raucous-voiced children played and shouted, and stared at Quest as he made his way down the street.

At forty-five the detective stopped and rapped with his knuckles at the dingy and broken door. At his third knock there came a shuffling of slippered feet from the passage inside and a slatternly woman opened the door a few inches and peered out.

'Go away,' she snapped. 'Don't want to buy nothin'.'

She tried to slam the door but Quest pressed his foot against it.

'I'm not selling anything,' he explained. 'I just want to have a word or two with you, if you're the landlady.'

The woman's pressure on the door relaxed and she opened it a trifle wider.

'Wotcher want with me, mister?' she enquired suspiciously.

Philip Quest produced a ten-shilling note from his pocket and held it ostentatiously in his fingers.

'You had staying with you some weeks ago a man called Deering,' he began. 'I want to ask you one or two questions concerning him.'

The woman eyed the note in the detective's hand greedily.

'Come into the 'all,' she invited more civilly.

Quest stepped inside the grimy and evil-smelling passage.

'I can't tell yer much about 'im,' she continued. ''E 'ad the attic at the top. 'E kept 'isself to 'isself, though 'e did give me a lot h'of bother dyin' sudden like that. What with doctors and policemen and inquests an' such like. What would yer be wanting to know, mister? You ain't the first person what's been h'enquirin' about 'im,' she added.

'Oh,' said Quest, a gleam of interest in his eyes. 'Who else has been making enquiries?'

'An old gent came about three days after 'e died,' said the woman, 'and wanted ter know this, that and the other. All sorts of questions 'e arst.'

'Did he say who he was?' asked the detective.

'Only that 'e 'ad been a friend of 'is,' said the landlady.

'Did Deering have many visitors?' asked Quest.

The woman shook her head.

'No,' she answered. 'There was an elderly man what come to see 'im once — not the same as was arstin' all the

84

questions — and once a young lady called.'

'What was the young lady like?' said Quest quickly.

'Oh, she was a real lady,' said the woman. 'Give me 'alf a dollar she did' — apparently the woman considered this a guarantee that she was a lady — 'fair she was an' pretty with big blue eyes like a baby's.'

It was a description that fitted Audrey Nesbitt.

'Did she mention her name?' queried the detective.

'No,' replied the woman. 'She wasn't 'ere more than five minutes.'

'You say she only came once?'

'That's h'all!'

'Did Deering receive many letters?'

'No,' she answered. ''E used to 'ave one what was printed now and again.'

'You mean typewritten?' asked the detective, and the woman nodded.

'Have you any idea where they came from or who sent them?'

She shook her head.

Quest felt that he was drawing a blank,

when, after a slight pause, she spoke again.

'H'i posted a parcel for 'im once,' she vouchsafed. ''E was too ill to go h'out 'isself an' 'e said it was h'urgent.'

Quest felt a little thrill go through him at the woman's words. A parcel! Could it be the mysterious box that the 'Devil's Dozen' had risked so much to obtain?

'What sort of parcel?' he enquired.

'H'it were about a foot square,' replied the landlady, 'an' 'eavy — seemed a sort of box.'

'Do you remember who it was addressed to?' asked Philip Quest.

She nodded her untidy head vigorously.

'Yes,' she answered. 'To a Miss Audrey Nesbitt, care of Sir Lionel Trevor, at some number h'in Portman Square!'

5

A Call in the night

It was in a very thoughtful mood that Philip Quest made his way back to his office, after leaving the dilapidated house in Lambeth.

The woman's words had come as a surprise, but not such a startling one as might be imagined, for the detective had previously had a vague suspicion concerning the truth that her statement had merely confirmed.

In Kennington Road he hailed a taxi and as he drove swiftly along he turned over in his mind the events of the day.

It seemed that the mysterious box, which appeared to be at the root of the affair, had never been sent to Sir Lionel Trevor at all, but to Audrey Nesbitt. Yet, under Quest's questioning the girl had denied all knowledge of it. He had been convinced at the time that she had been lying, and his visit to Gall Street had proved it beyond doubt.

She had also lied when she had stated that she did not know Deering, and had never heard the name before, for it was fairly obvious, from the landlady's description, that it was Audrey Nesbitt who had on one occasion called to see Deering. Taken in conjunction with the fact that she was the person to whom Deering had addressed the parcel, there could be no doubt whatever that they had been acquainted.

Why had the girl lied? Obviously she must have had some very good reason for wishing to conceal the fact that she had any connection with Deering. Was it possible that she had been the person who had broken into Sir Lionel Trevor's house and ransacked the study? If so, what could her object have been, for it was absurd to suppose that she was searching for a box which, according to the landlady, must have already been in her possession?

If she was the night intruder then Quest was wrong in supposing that the object of the burglary had been the box, and if not the box, what was it the 'Devil's Dozen' were looking for?

As far as he and Johnson had been able to ascertain, nothing had apparently been stolen, but then, only Sir Lionel was in a position to state exactly what had been in the study, and he was dead. There might quite easily be some paper or papers missing which they knew nothing about.

If the girl had been the person who had broken in, then it was only logical to suppose that she was also guilty of the murder, and Quest could not bring himself to believe that.

His keen brain had already formed a theory to account for the thread of black silk, which he had found adhering to Sir Lionel's finger nail, a more feasible theory, he believed, than that it had come from the silk coat Audrey Nesbitt had been wearing.

If his idea was the right one then the only fact that proved that the girl had been present when Sir Lionel had met his death was of no evidential value.

It was a puzzling problem, one of the

most puzzling that the detective had ever tackled. The more so as there was practically nothing to go on, not a vestige of a clue that would lead him to the identity of the murderer.

Although there was no doubt that the 'Devil's Dozen' were behind the affair, the organisation was so illusive, such a thing of intangible shadows, that his resolve to run them to earth appeared to be an impossible task.

Ever since the gang had first sprung into prominence, which was nearly eight months previously, Philip Quest had used every endeavour, strained every nerve, to track them down, but without success.

The central figure of the gang, that mysterious and illusive being who successfully cloaked his identity under the soubriquet of the 'Stranger,' had frustrated every attempt on the part of Quest and the police to lift the veil that shrouded his activities. In every crime committed by the 'Devil's Dozen,' and there had been many, the preliminary organisation had been so perfect, and in each case every detail so carefully planned, that not the slightest trace of a clue had ever been left.

Whoever the leader was, and Quest was determined to unmask him and bring him to justice, the detective had to admit that he was a criminal genius. He seemed to be possessed of an uncanny faculty of knowing in advance every move made against him.

Another point that clearly connected Audrey Nesbitt with the 'Devil's Dozen' was the fact that according to Lester she had been present that morning at the trial of Jefferson Harlowe. Why had she been there?

Harlowe, it was true, was a member of the 'Devil's Dozen,' and it was possible that she had only gone out of mere idle curiosity, but at the same time there might have been a deeper reason, and if so, what could it be?

Quest was still determined to prove, if possible, that Harlowe was the victim of a 'frame up,' as he suspected. But who could have been responsible for the 'frame up?' It was either just an act of petty spite or the result of a carefully laid plan, and if the latter, must have been conceived by someone who knew that Harlowe was going to be at Benson's office at that exact time. But who could have been certain of this fact? Obviously the man who, if Harlowe had been speaking the truth, had instructed him to be there — the 'Stranger.'

The only conclusion to be drawn from this was that the man who had sent the telephone warning to Scotland Yard and the 'Stranger' were one and the same. But if this was the case, what was the object?

A vague idea began to form itself in Quest's keen, alert brain. An idea that seemed at first so fantastic that for a moment he hardly allowed himself to give it credence.

He was still turning it over in his mind when the taxi drew up at his office in the city, and the detective got out. He was still thinking deeply as he absently fitted his key in the lock.

His investigation at Portman Square and his subsequent enquiries at Lambeth had occupied a considerable time and it was past six when he entered the consulting-room.

Norman Carfax was sitting in a chair by the cosy fire, and rose to greet him as he entered.

'I hope you didn't mind me waiting,' he said, as he shook hands with the detective. 'Your maid said she didn't know what time you'd be back so I thought I'd wait for you, on the off-chance you might be early.'

Quest waved him back into the chair and crossed to the mantelpiece and took a cigarette from the box which stood there.

'I am very glad to see you,' he said as he felt in his pocket for the matches.

'It's a dreadful business about Sir Lionel, Quest,' said Carfax. 'A dreadful business. I knew him well, he was a great friend of mine. I came round directly I saw the news in the paper. Have you discovered anything that is likely to lead to the identity of his murderer?'

Before replying Philip Quest lit his cigarette and blew a cloud of smoke ceilingwards.

'I only know that the 'Devil's Dozen'

are at the bottom of it,' he answered. 'And as usual they've left no clue behind them.'

Carfax struck his knee with his open hand impatiently.

'Can nothing be done to put an end to this menace? It is striking at the root of the whole of civilisation. These people seem to do exactly as they like without anybody being able to prevent them. They are making all the traditions of law and authority a laughing stock. Nobody knows who they are. They come from nowhere, commit some audacious crime, and vanish again into the shadows from which they came. The police have proved themselves helpless, Quest, but surely something can be done?'

'The only thing that can be done, my dear Carfax,' said Quest quietly, as he sank into a chair opposite the other, 'is to find the 'Stranger.' Find him and the rest of the gang will take care of themselves. Without their leader they would not last five minutes.'

'But how are you going to find him?' asked Carfax. 'Nobody knows who he is, not even the members of his own gang.

You know what Harlowe said. All the instructions he received were typewritten and posted to him. He only saw the man who sent them once, and beyond the fact that he wore a mask and was bearded, he can give no description. There is nothing at all to go on.'

Philip Quest was silent, his eyes half closed.

'The 'Stranger' will make a slip sooner or later, Carfax,' he murmured after a while. 'All criminals do. It may be a little one or it may be a big one, but sooner or later he will make it and then we've got him.'

'I hope you're right, Quest,' said Carfax earnestly. 'I would give a lot to bring the murderer of my poor friend to justice. What reason could they have had for killing Trevor?'

'Because he interrupted the intruder during his search,' replied Quest. 'That's my own idea.'

'Was anything stolen?' asked Carfax. 'The report I read in the papers was very vague, just a short paragraph.'

'As far as I can tell at the moment,'

replied the detective, 'nothing appears to be stolen.'

'What could have been their object in breaking in then?' demanded Carfax.

'I believe they were searching for a certain box,' replied Quest, and he briefly related the contents of the half-burnt letter found by Johnson in the grate.

Carfax listened interestedly.

'You don't know whether they got what they were looking for or not?' he asked, when the detective had finished.

Quest shook his head.

'I was inclined to believe they had at first,' he replied slowly. 'But my subsequent enquiries at Lambeth have made me alter my opinion, because undoubtedly the box was never sent to Sir Lionel at all. That's where they must have got their information wrong. It was certainly sent to his house but it was addressed to his secretary, Miss Nesbitt.'

'What in the world can it contain,' said Carfax wrinkling his forehead in perplexity.

'I haven't the least idea, Carfax,' replied Quest candidly. 'It must be of immense value either to the gang or to the 'Stranger' for them to take so much trouble to obtain it.'

'Have you any idea, Quest,' asked Carfax after a slight pause, 'or any suspicion as to who this mysterious individual can be?'

Quest removed his cigarette from between his lips and blew out a cloud of smoke before replying.

'No,' he answered, 'not the slightest. I don't think he is anyone known to the police. I have been through all the records of every known criminal I could possibly think of and discarded them all in the end. There is only one man among them who, as far as I know, possesses sufficient brains to have made a success of an organisation like the 'Devil's Dozen,' and he is at present serving a sentence of fifteen years for blackmail. No,' he continued absently, staring up at the ceiling, 'I feel that the 'Stranger' is an entirely new figure in the annals of crime, and I don't mind betting that when he is finally unmasked, we are all going to get a big surprise.'

'Well, I hope I am there,' said Carfax,

'when you run him to earth. I am as much interested as you are, Quest, and I hope you'll let me know if I can do anything to help.' He glanced at the clock and rose to his feet. 'By Jove! I'd no idea it was so late,' he exclaimed. 'I must be off now, I have got a brief to look into for to-morrow which is rather intricate.'

For some time after he had gone Philip Quest remained staring into the fire, then he rose and crossed to the door leading into his bedroom. When he returned he was clad in an old comfortable dressing-gown, and settled himself down to a few hours of concentrated thought, during which time he weighed all the points of the problem, sorting and resorting the facts until he had selected those which he considered were essential to the solving of the puzzle.

In this case, however, there were so few clues to work on, so little information at his command, try as he would, he could not hit upon any point that was likely to lead him to the truth. Hunched up in his favourite armchair, the cigarette box close to his hand, oblivious alike of time and place, he sat motionless, his eyes closed.

The only sign of life that he exhibited was a steady stream of smoke from the countless cigarettes he smoked.

For two hours he sat thus, disturbed once only when the maid put her head round the corner of the door to announce that dinner was ready. She might as well have been speaking to a brick wall for all her master took notice, and knowing his moods, she tiptoed quietly away, shaking her head in despair, for she knew from experience that the dinner that had so carefully been prepared was going to be wasted.

At nine o'clock a messenger arrived from Scotland Yard with the Records of Deering that Johnson had promised to send round. They were contained in a bulky envelope, and after the messenger had gone Quest perused the contents. With an open notebook on his knee he went carefully through them, making extracts which appeared to him to have a bearing on the matter in hand.

There were several pages of information concerning Deering's past life, and here Quest found one paragraph that interested him considerably.

It stated that Deering at one time was believed to have been at Oxford. Beside this was a note in a neat hand in red ink briefly stating:

'This has been enquired into but no trace can be found to substantiate the information received.'

It was nearly half-past ten before he had finally finished, and crossing to his desk, he sat down and wrote a long letter to an agent of his who lived at Oxford, enclosing the notes that he had made from Deering's record. Having stamped and sealed the letter, the detective returned to his chair.

There was nothing to do now but wait Lester's return from the shadowing of Audrey Nesbitt, on the chance that he would have some information that might add to Quest's meagre store of facts.

That the girl was deeply concerned in the affair he was certain, and so he hoped that through her he would eventually find the clue which he sought, that would lead him to the solution of the mystery surrounding the identity of the 'Stranger.'

The time went on but there was no sign of Lester, and as it got later and later Quest began to feel a vague uneasiness. Could it be possible that something had happened to him? The detective was well aware that they were dealing with a desperate gang who would stick at nothing to maintain their safety, and Lester was famous for getting himself into a tight corner. True he had, so far, always managed to wriggle out again, but there was always the possibility of a time when he might go a step too far.

As the hours passed by Quest's uneasiness increased. Surely he ought to have had a message from Lester by now. He commenced to pace the room with long, nervous strides. Again and again he told himself that his fears were ground-less, that nothing had happened, that Lester was still engaged in watching the house in Bloomsbury.

He knew his partner too well to believe that he would return until he had exhausted every chance of discovering some fresh information, but although he tried to re-assure himself, he knew that he was wrong. Some instinct, a vague intuition, warned him of danger. Twice he almost made up his mind to go to Bloomsbury and see if Lester was still there, but each time reason asserted itself and he saw the folly of such a course.

If Lester was still there he was certainly not in any danger, and if on the other hand he had gone, it was next to impossible for Quest to trace him. There was nothing for it but to wait as calmly as possible for news from his partner himself.

The little clock on the mantelpiece presently chimed out the hour of twelve, and Quest, with a little impatient gesture, crushed out his cigarette and decided to go to bed.

It was some time before he fell asleep but eventually he dropped into a fitful doze. It seemed to have lasted barely five minutes when he was startled into an abrupt wakefulness by the shrill ringing of the telephone bell. The hands of the clock by his side pointed to a few minutes past three.

'It must be a message from Lester at last,' he thought, as he picked up the receiver. But it wasn't.

A man's voice came over the wire, a strange voice, full of agitation and alarm.

'Is that Mr. Philip Quest?' it asked.

Quest replied in the affirmative.

'Mr. Carfax wants to speak to you,' the voice continued. 'Will you hold the line a moment.'

Presently Quest heard Carfax's voice at the other end.

'Hello, Quest,' he cried. 'Can you come round to my flat in Ryder Street at once?'

'Why?' asked the detective. 'What's the matter?'

'The 'Devil's Dozen' have turned their attention to me!' he said excitedly. 'The place was broken into half an hour ago, turned upside down and thoroughly ransacked!'

'How do you know it was the 'Devil's Dozen'?' asked Quest, his pulses thrilling slightly.

'They left a card,' was the surprising reply. 'An ordinary visiting-card with 'The Stranger' scrawled across it in pencil!'

6

A Mysterious Attack

Quest dressed in record time, and was lucky enough to find a belated taxi, and in less than half an hour of receiving the telephone message he arrived at Carfax's flat in Ryder Street. The flat was situated in a large block, the big entrance was brilliantly lit as the detective drove up and sprang out of the cab.

As Quest entered a man dressed in a porter's uniform emerged from a glass panelled, box-like apartment in one corner and accosted him.

'Are you the gentleman Mr. Carfax is expecting?' he asked.

Quest nodded, and the man led the way towards a lift. Carfax's fiat was on the third floor.

'This is a nice business,' grumbled the man as they went swiftly upwards. 'The first case of burglary here, and it won't do

104

the flats any good, I can tell you.' He opened the door when they reached the third landing, and Quest stepped out. 'Mr. Carfax's flat is on the right,' he said, touching his cap.

Philip Quest hurried to the door, beneath the knocker of which was a small brass plate bearing the name of Norman Carfax, and rang the bell.

In answer to his ring the door was opened by a man servant, an elderly, agitated man, half dressed, who had been visibly upset by the night's events, for his hand trembled violently as he took the detective's hat and gloves.

Carfax himself appeared almost at the same moment, dressed in a resplendent silk dressing-gown which he had evidently pulled on hurriedly over his pyjamas.

'I'm glad you have come, Quest,' he greeted. 'Sorry to have pulled you out in the middle of the night, but I knew you would be interested.'

'Have you informed the police?' asked Quest.

Carfax shook his head.

'Not yet,' he said. 'I thought you would

prefer to have a look round first. Come into the study.'

He opened a door on the left of the tiny hall and led the way into a big, comfortably-furnished room, half library and half sitting room.

The main article of furniture was a large leather-topped writing-table, which occupied the recess of the window overlooking the street.

As in the case of Sir Lionel's study, the room was in the utmost disorder, papers and books had been flung in every direction; the drawers of the writing-table pulled out and emptied. A cupboard which occupied one corner had been forced open and the contents littered the carpet.

'They made a pretty good job of it, didn't they,' said Carfax ruefully, as they surveyed the wreckage. 'What beats me is what the object could have been.'

'Anything stolen?' asked Philip Quest, his keen eyes travelling swiftly round the dismantled room.

'I haven't had time to make sure yet,' replied Carfax. 'I phoned you directly we discovered that somebody had broken in.'

'How did you first discover it?' asked the detective.

'There was a noise like a door slamming that wakened me,' said Carfax. 'I came down at once to see what had happened, and found the light on and the place like this.'

'Do you know how they got in?' asked Quest, his eyes darting backward and forward.

Carfax nodded.

'Up the fire escape and through the window of a small room at the back,' he replied. 'We don't use it, it's practically a store room and the fire escape runs almost level with the window. The window was open and the latch had been forced back.'

'Where does the fire escape lead to?' asked Quest.

'Down into a courtyard at the back of the building,' replied Carfax.

'Any means of getting into the courtyard from the street?'

'Yes, there's a door that leads into a narrow alley, and from thence into a road that runs almost parallel with Ryder Street.'

Quest surveyed the room in silence for several seconds, then he turned to Carfax.

'You'd better make sure if anything has been stolen while I take a look round,' he said quietly. He crossed over to the writing table by the window and carefully examined the drawers which had been forced open. 'Whoever opened these drawers,' he remarked a moment later, 'was certainly an amateur at the game. The job has been very clumsily carried out. Where is the card you said was left behind?'

Carfax, who was trying to arrange the papers on the floor into something resembling order, looked up.

'It's on the writing table, Quest,' he said. 'On the top of the paper weight.'

Quest found the card, and picking it up looked at it intently, tapping his chin thoughtfully with his long forefinger. It was an ordinary visiting card of the type that can be bought at any stationers', and the signature had been scrawled across it hurriedly in pencil. The detective held it carefully by the edges.

'The police will want to test this card for finger-prints,' he said. 'Though I doubt very much if they will find any. The 'Devil's Dozen' are too clever for that.'

Presently he put it down on the paper weight where he had found, it. An exclamation from Carfax caused him to turn quickly.

'I say, Quest,' he cried excitedly, 'I've found something.'

The detective stepped over to where he was kneeling beside the papers that were strewn on the floor by the cupboard.

'I found this on the floor,' continued Carfax, and held out a small white object.

Quest took it and examined it under the white light of the light which hung from the centre of the ceiling. It was a silk handkerchief, edged with lace, and a woman's. As the criminologist turned it over in his slim fingers he saw that the initials of the owner had been embroidered in mauve silk in one corner.

A little gleam crept into his eyes as he made out the monogram A.N. — Audrey Nesbitt!

Carfax had risen to his feet and was standing by the detective's elbow, eyeing the handkerchief with interest.

'Is that any clue, Quest?' he asked.

Philip Quest pointed silently to the initials in the corner.

'A.N.,' said Carfax, in a puzzled voice, then suddenly: 'By Jove! that stands for the name of the girl to whom you told me Deering sent the box.'

Quest nodded slowly, his keen brain was briskly working. In both cases the only clue he had been able to obtain had pointed directly to the girl.

'Can it be possible, Quest,' cried Carfax excitedly, 'that the leader of the 'Devil's Dozen' is a woman?'

'It's possible,' replied the detective, 'but I hardly think it is probable. No woman, however clever, would be able to control an organisation like the 'Devil's Dozen,' and certainly no woman as young as Audrey Nesbitt is. No, Carfax, I don't know how she fits into the affair but I am certain that she is not the 'Stranger'.' He slipped the handkerchief into his pocket. 'I am going to have a look at the room by which you say the intruder gained access.'

'Collins will show yon the way.' said Carfax, and rang the bell.

The man-servant who had let Quest in answered the summons, and at a word from Carfax led the detective down a short corridor, at the end of which was an open door leading into a tiny room, scarcely bigger than a large cupboard.

It was filled with trunks and suit-cases and the odds and ends which usually accumulate in a lumber room. The man-servant pointed out a tiny window through which the midnight visitor was believed to have entered, and would have withdrawn if Quest had not stopped him.

'What do you know about this affair?' he asked. 'Did you hear anything in the night?'

Collins shook his head.

'No, sir,' he replied. 'I didn't know there was anything wrong until I found Mr. Carfax standing at my bedside, shaking me by the shoulder.'

'You heard no noise prior to that?' asked Quest.

'Nothing, sir,' answered the man.

Quest nodded a dismissal, and turned his attention to the window.

The latch was an old one and had been forced back with some sharp instrument which had left a scratch upon the hasp. Resting his hands on the inside of the sill the detective leaned out. The iron staircase of the fire escape ran so near that, without leaning very far, he could touch it with his fingers. It would have been an easy matter for anyone to have stepped from thence on to the sill. Quest drew his electric torch from his pocket and carefully examined the window sill. A thin sooty film covered the stone, a film that the smoky atmosphere of London desposits everywhere, and printed in the dust was a small, circular mark, the heel print of a woman's high-heeled shoe!

The detective's breath hissed gently through his teeth as he saw it. There could be little doubt that the night visitor to Carfax's flat had been a woman, and still less that that woman was Audrey Nesbitt. Had she come in company with the 'Stranger' or had she come alone? If she had come alone, how was it possible to account for the card being found on the desk, unless the girl had left it there herself? Was Carfax right in his theory that Audrey Nesbitt was the leader of the 'Devil's Dozen.' Everything seemed to point to the fact, and yet Quest was convinced in his own mind that this was an impossibility.

If it had been she who had broken into Carfax's flat where was Lester, for he had been instructed to watch the girl and follow her wherever she went. In that case he must have followed her to the flat, and why had he not sent a message to him to inform him of the fact. The whole thing was most puzzling, and Quest gave it up and returned to the study.

He found that during his absence Carfax had reduced the litter to something like order.

'There's nothing of value missing, Quest,' said Carfax as the detective entered, 'only an envelope containing some of my notes on the Harlowe case.'

'The Harlowe case,' repeated Quest thoughtfully. 'Are you sure that's all that has been taken?'

Carfax nodded.

'What use that could have been to the 'Devil's Dozen,' I'm hanged if I know,' he answered.

Philip Quest was about to reply when his eye caught sight of something that lay in the shadow of the writing table, something that was green and struck a bright note of colour on the grey carpet. It must have been invisible from where Carfax stood, and swiftly crossing the room the detective stooped and picked it up.

It was a cloak room ticket, the kind of ticket that is received in exchange for luggage at a station, and it was stamped Victoria. He held it out to Carfax.

'Is this yours?' he enquired.

Carfax looked at it a moment and then shook his head.

'No, it's not mine,' he answered.

'Would it belong to anyone in the flat?' asked Quest.

'There's only Collins here,' said Carfax, 'and I'm sure it doesn't belong to him.'

'Ask him,' said Quest briefly.

Carfax summoned his man-servant, but

he could give them no information concerning the ticket.

'It obviously must have been dropped by the person who broke in,' said Quest, when, the man had gone. 'It is the first tangible clue we have got hold of so far, and it has obviously been received in exchange for a suit-case and an examination of that suitcase will, in all probability, afford us some means of identifying the owner. There is nothing more I can do here, Carfax,' he added. 'The best thing you can do is to inform the police. I'm going back to my place now.'

Quest was anxious to return in case there should be a message from Lester, for he was becoming seriously alarmed at his partner's continued absence.

Dawn was breaking as he left the block of flats in Ryder Street and the detective decided to walk back to his flat in the cool sweet air of the morning. He set off at a swinging pace, covering the ground with long easy strides. His sense of direction was mechanical, his mind was busy with the strange problem which he had set himself to solve, for Philip Quest's keen eyes had discovered a clue of which he had said nothing to Carfax.

So occupied was he with his own thoughts that he failed to notice the large limousine car that was crawling along in his wake, and even had he done so it is doubtful whether he would have taken much notice of it. The car followed about two hundred yards behind, and as the detective swung out of Regent Street into Oxford Street it put on speed and drew almost level with him.

He became aware of its presence almost at the same instant, and as he turned there came two sharp reports almost simultaneously from the driver's seat.

The detective collapsed on the pavement without a sound, and the car, gathering speed, quickly disappeared in the direction of Marble Arch, leaving behind it a little wreath of blue grey smoke that hung motionless in the still morning air over the inert body of Philip Quest!

7

Lester's Vigil

Richard Lester in the meanwhile on leaving Portman Square, made his way as quickly as possible to Bloomsbury and found no difficulty in locating the house in which Audrey Nesbitt lived.

It was situated on the extreme corner of a street leading off the far end of Russell Square, a big, ugly-looking house; one of those building with which the streets in this part of London abound.

At one time a private house, it had degenerated into a boarding-house, and had eventually been sold and converted by its new owner into self-contained flats.

By the side of the green-painted main door were a row of bell pushes, beside which was a corresponding name plate to each, so that Lester experienced no trouble in discovering the flat occupied by the girl.

It was on the second floor, and Audrey Nesbitt was apparently at home, for there was a light in her window and as he made a swift inspection of the house on passing he saw the shadow of her slim figure silhouetted against the blind as she moved across the room.

Dusk had already fallen when he arrived and a sharp frost was visible in the shape of a thin white mist that struck cold and chill and caused Lester to shiver slightly. He walked on to the end of the street, and crossing the road, prepared to retrace his steps on the opposite side. As he strolled slowly back his eyes roamed hither and thither seeking a likely place from whence he could command a view of the house without making himself too conspicuous.

Presently he found what he wanted. Over by the railings that surrounded the gardens in the centre of Russell Square was a cab rank, on which four or five taxis were waiting, and Lester decided that it would be an ideal spot to take up his position, for under cover of the cabs he could watch the entrance to the flats without risk of being seen and recognised by Audrey Nesbitt, should the girl come out.

He lounged slowly over and prepared to stroll casually up and down as though waiting to keep an appointment. He had passed a little group of taxi drivers who were leaning against the railings chatting and smoking, when he felt a touch on his arm and swung round.

One of the men had detached himself from the others and was standing by his elbow.

'I thought it was you, sir,' he said, touching his cap as Lester turned. 'You remember me, don't you, Ainsley, sir. It's Mr. Lester, ain't it?'

Lester recognised the man at once.

He was a taxi man named Jim Ainsley, who had often driven Philip Quest and himself, and for some time had occupied a rank in Holborn. He was well known to both the detective and his assistant.

'Hello, Ainsley,' said Lester, and in a moment of recognising the man an idea had been born in his alert brain. 'I'm jolly glad you happen to be here, you can help me. Which is your cab?'

The man pointed to the last one on the rank.

'Well, listen,' continued Lester. 'I want to keep an eye on that house over there. Can I sit in your cab? I will pay you, of course.'

'Sure,' assented the driver, readily, 'never mind the payment, sir. I'm always willing to do anything I can for you or Mr. Quest.'

He led the way over to the cab and opened the door.

'Jump in, sir.'

Lester slipped into the dark interior and peered out of the window. As a place of vantage it could not be improved on, for he could command a clear view of the corner house and the steps leading to the front door. No one could enter or leave the house without Lester seeing them, for a street lamp on the corner had just been lighted and threw a bright splash of radiance under which anyone going or coming from the house would have to pass. Also he was already provided with the means of pursuit should his quarry take a cab.

Jim Ainsley shut the door and touching his cap climbed into the driver's seat, lit the stub of a cigarette which he took from behind his ear, and producing an evening paper settled down to read, while Lester prepared himself for his vigil.

The hours dragged slowly by and nothing happened. The windows of Audrey Nesbitt's flat still remained lighted, but beyond that there had been no sign of movement from the girl.

Seven o'clock struck and Lester was beginning to get decidedly fed up. His adventurous soul demanded action. He was feeling in the mood for some excitement, anything that would break the dreadful monotony of this waiting game which his impetuous nature hated.

Had he realised what lay in store for him before the night was through he would not have been so discontented, for he was to pass through a time with enough excitement and peril to appeal to even his craving for adventure.

Eight o'clock struck and as the last notes died away on the still night air the lights in Audrey Nesbitt's flat suddenly went out. Was the girl about to come out, thought Lester or had she merely gone to bed early?

He was soon to know, for presently the front door opened and she appeared on the top of the steps, and the next moment was hurrying off in the direction of Southampton Row.

Lester slipped from the cab, hastily thrust a ten-shilling note in Jim Ainsley's hand, and set off in pursuit. The girl was walking quickly and it was evident from her movements that she was bound to keep an appointment, for every now and again she glanced at the little watch on her wrist. Down Southampton Row, past the corner of Theobolds Road and so on into Kingsway she went, with Lester close at her heels. Presently she reached the Strand and waited at a bus stop. A bus bound for Piccadilly Circus soon rolled up and the girl boarded it, going inside. Lester did likewise, but went to the top, taking a seat from which he could command a view of anyone getting on or off.

He only glanced casually at the elderly bearded man who followed him up the steps and took a seat in front of him, but later he was to have good cause to remember him.

At Piccadilly Circus the girl alighted, and followed by Lester, made her way across to the Tube Station, where she stopped and looked about, evidently in search of someone.

Lester took up his stand outside the London Pavilion, for there he could keep an eye on the girl without risk of being seen by her himself. Presently he saw his fellow passenger, the grey-bearded, elderly man, walk slowly past the girl and stop at the corner of the Haymarket.

Lester became interested. Was it possible that someone else was following Audrey Nesbitt besides himself? He put the idea out of his mind as soon as he thought of it. Of course it was only a coincidence that the bearded man had travelled on the same bus, and was now waiting outside the Tube Station. That particular point was a meeting place for thousands of people, but still there was no harm, thought the young man, in keeping an eye on the stranger.

About five minutes passed and then a young man came hurrying out of the Tube and approached the girl, raising his hat. They stood talking for a moment and then moved off towards Coventry Street. Lester followed on the opposite side of the road, they passed the bearded stranger on the corner and a few minutes after he, too, strolled leisurely off in their wake.

Richard Lester felt a little thrill run through him. There was now little doubt that his first surmise had been correct and that he was not the only one who was interested in Audrey Nesbitt's movements. The evening promised more excitement than he had expected.

The girl and her companion paused opposite Lyons' Corner House and then crossed the road. As they moved into the glare of the light outside the front, Lester, for the first time, caught a clear view of the face of the young man who accompanied her. It was with a little start of surprise that he recognised him, for it was Jack Archer, Charles Benson's late secretary!

There was no possible doubt of it for he had seen him several times in court during the trial of Jefferson Harlowe.

What possible connection could there be between Audrey Nesbitt and the murdered man's secretary?

They passed in through the entrance to the big tea shop and went through to the all-night café at the back. Lester waited for a moment, gazing in the window, trying to make up his mind what he should do next. If he followed them there was every chance that in the brilliantly lit interior Audrey Nesbitt would recognise him, and that was the last thing that he wanted to happen. On the other hand, if he waited it was quite likely that they would leave by another exit, in which case he would lose sight of the girl altogether.

Lester decided to risk it, and pulling his hat well down over his eyes, prepared to follow his quarry.

He was in the act of entering when the grey-bearded man pushed past him and hurried through in the wake of Audrey

Nesbitt and her companion. If Richard Lester had had any remaining doubt before that the grey-bearded man was trailing the girl and Jack Archer, the fact of the man following them into the tea shop was sufficient to convince him that his first suspicions were correct.

Lester glanced round as he entered and presently made out Audrey Nesbitt and Archer; they had secured a table (practically the only one vacant) over by the quick lunch counter at the far end and were engaged in an animated conversation, or rather the girl was, for she appeared to be doing all the talking and accompanied her words with little quick, excited gestures.

He saw at once that it was hopeless for him to get near enough to overhear what they were saying, and he contented himself by dropping into a vacant seat from which he could at least keep them in sight. Having sat down he looked round to see what had become of the grey-bearded man, and saw him searching for a place to sit.

Eventually he found a table by the

entrance. It was already occupied by a little party of foreigners, but there was one chair vacant and on this the grey-bearded man seated himself.

Lester was now able to take stock of his appearance. He was rather shabbily dressed in an overcoat of some dark material, the collar of which was turned up about his neck. A grey felt hat rested rather low over his eyes so that very little of his face was visible, and what there was was almost entirely covered by the grey, straggling beard and moustache which almost covered the mouth and chin. He had turned his chair so that he could obtain a view of the girl and her companion, and Lester noticed that his eyes were fixed intently upon them, from under the brim of his hat.

Lester wondered who he was and what his object could be in shadowing the girl. Was he a member of the 'Devil's Dozen' who was waiting an opportunity to communicate with her. He thought it was scarcely possible, for if so he would have had ample opportunity to do so either before she boarded the bus in the Strand or during the journey to Piccadilly. That the girl was totally unaware of his presence he was also certain for she never even once glanced in his direction. Try as he might he could not find a place for this mysterious stranger in the scheme of things.

The girl and Jack Archer had ordered coffee and were still deep in conversation, but now it was the young man who was doing all the talking, and he appeared to be arguing, for every now and again in answer to something he said, the girl shook her head decisively, at which he leaned forward earnestly and continued his argument most emphatically, evidently trying vainly to make her see his point of view.

For over an hour they continued thus and Lester was beginning to wonder what the next move would be when suddenly the girl rose to her feet and looked at her watch. The young man laid a hand on her arm, apparently trying to detain her, but she gently shook it off, again shaking her head, and with a resigned shrug of his shoulders he also rose to his feet and signalled to the waitress for his bill. Lester waited until they had passed the pay desk and then obtained his bill and followed.

At Piccadilly Circus Audrey Nesbitt left her companion and presently boarded a bus travelling towards the Strand. Lester slipped on the bus as it was passing, and as before made his way to the top.

He glanced round as he sat down to see if there were any signs of the bearded man, but he had apparently vanished. There was little doubt, thought Lester, that the girl was now going back home, and he began to wish that he had transferred his attentions from Audrey Nesbitt to the man with the beard.

At the same spot where she had boarded the previous bus the girl got down and proceeded to walk swiftly up the Kingsway towards Russell Square.

Lester, feeling thoroughly fed up with the apparently tame ending to an evening that had one time promised some excitement, followed. There was still the chance, a very slender one, he thought, that she wasn't going directly home, but in this he was to be disappointed, for she made straight for Russell Square and shortly after he watched her ascend the steps of the block of flats and let herself in with a key.

Now he was undecided what to do. Should he go back to his partner and report what had happened or should he hang around on the chance of something further occurring? It was getting late and there seemed little chance of the girl coming out again, but at the same time he had nothing much to tell Quest, and Lester felt strongly disinclined to go back to him with the small amount of information he had so far acquired.

He decided at length to stick it out a little longer, and with this object commenced to stroll leisurely up and down the side street on the corner of which the block of flats was situated.

The street was very quiet and deserted and the thin white mist which had been barely noticeable earlier in the evening had got thicker.

He wished with all his heart that he had followed the bearded man, for he felt sure that by doing so he would have had more chance of discovering some useful information than by hanging about watching a block of flats, which seemed to him to be merely a waste of time.

He had almost reached the end of the street and had decided to turn back and retrace his steps when the sound of a soft footfall behind him caused him to swing round, but he was too late! There came a sudden rush of running footsteps; a figure loomed out of the darkness, and before Richard Lester had time to defend himself something soft and heavy descended with a crushing force on his head, a fiery curtain flashed before his eyes and he remembered no more!

8

Philip Quest's Startling Discovery

Philip Quest opened his eyes to discover a policeman bending anxiously over him. His head was throbbing painfully and he felt dazed and a trifle sick.

'What happened, sir?' exclaimed the man as Quest sat up gingerly. 'I heard the sound of shots and came along to see what was the matter, and found you lying on the pavement.'

Quest pressed a hand to his aching head, and his fingers came away from his forehead wet and sticky.

'Somebody in a car tried to shoot me, Constable,' he murmured, 'but I don't think they have done much damage, apparently the bullet has only grazed the side of my head. It was enough to stun me for the moment, but I am all right now.'

With the help of the policeman's arm

he rose shakily to his feet.

'Do you know who it was, sir?' asked the constable, producing a notebook from the pocket of his tunic.

The detective started to shake his head, but the movement caused him such acute agony that he refrained.

'I haven't the least idea,' he replied. 'I didn't get a chance to catch a glance of whoever it was, they were in a closed car.'

The constable looked at him a little suspiciously.

'I shall have to ask you for your name and address, sir,' he said.

'My name is Philip Quest,' answered the detective, and feeling in his pocket he produced a card case and handed the constable a card.

The man's attitude changed as he heard the famous name.

'I'm glad to have had the pleasure of meeting you, Mr. Quest,' he said, gazing at the detective with something like awe in his eyes, 'although I could have wished that it had been under different circumstances. You say the shots were fired from a closed car, I suppose you didn't happen to see the number?'

'No,' replied Quest. 'It was all done so quickly that I hadn't the time to notice anything. Although I can't tell you the name of the attacker, I have a pretty shrewd idea that the 'Devil's Dozen' gang are at the bottom of it.'

'I have heard of them,' said the constable, as he made an entry in his notebook.

'You're likely to hear a great deal more of them before long,' replied Quest grimly.

Beyond a violent headache, he was feeling little the worse for his experience and after complying with the necessary formalities which were needed for the constable to make his report, Quest left the man, and continued on his way to his flat. The bullet had stripped a piece of skin from his forehead and the wound was bleeding profusely, and having improvised a rough bandage with his handkerchief, Quest decided to seek a chemist's to have it properly dressed.

He failed to satisfy the obvious curiosity of the man who bandaged the wound, and emerging from the shop, looked round for a taxi to take him home. Luckily there was a cab rank close at hand and within a few minutes he was bowling swiftly along in the direction of his home.

Immediately on arriving there he had a hot bath and a change and by then the pain had almost subsided. While he awaited breakfast he went over in his mind the events of the preceding night. The reason for the robbery at Carfax's flat was as much a mystery as that of the Portman Square affair; more so, since Quest was convinced in the latter case that the 'Devil's Dozen' had been searching for the box mentioned in the burnt letter, but in Carfax's case, however, there was nothing to suggest the reason for their breaking in. It was inconceivable to suppose that their object had been to obtain the notes on the Harlowe case which Carfax had declared was all that had been stolen.

But Quest had noticed something on entering the flat at Ryder Street, something that he had not remarked on to

Carfax, that had set his mind running on a theory so startling, so absolutely incredible, that he found it difficult even to admit of its possibility to himself. But it was there, an intangible thing it was true, and although it seemed too utterly preposterous to be given credence, it kept rising unbidden in his mind, and through its very persistence demanded to be taken notice of.

But at the moment the thing that worried him more than all was the continued absence of Lester. What could have happened to him? That something unforeseen had occurred he was certain. Was he hot on the trail of some new clue or had he run foul of the 'Stranger' and his terrible organisation? Quest was aware, if only from his experience that morning, that the gang would stick at nothing to preserve their own safety and if, during his shadowing of Audrey Nesbitt, Lester had stumbled on anything that might form a clue as to their identity and they had become aware of the fact his partner's chances of returning with his knowledge were remote.

He tried to switch his thoughts into another channel. Worrying about his friend would do no good, and for the time being at least he was powerless to take any action.

Who were the person or persons who had fired at him from the limousine? He had only managed to catch a faint glimpse of the driver, and the figure was so muffled up that it was impossible to distinguish whether it had been a man or a woman. Whoever it was, they must have known that he had gone to Ryder Street, and where had they got their information from? There was the possibility that they had been watching him, or had been still hanging about Carfax's flat when the detective had arrived.

The arrival of breakfast put an end to his conjectures and almost at the same moment that he sat down to the appetising dish of kidneys and bacon that had been prepared there came a ring at the bell, and shortly after Detective-Inspector Johnson was announced.

The burly Scotland Yard man growled out a greeting as he entered, and flung himself heavily into a chair.

'I've just heard the latest news, Quest,' he said, 'about Carfax, I mean. He rang up the Yard. As a matter of fact I have just come from his flat now. It seems to be a pretty rum go. What do you make of it?'

Philip Quest sipped at his coffee before replying.

'I have formed no theory at all, yet, Johnson,' he admitted, 'but the 'Devil's Dozen' certainly appear to be very much on the war-path. They nearly got me this, morning.'

Johnson sat bolt upright in his chair and stared at Quest in amazement.

'What do you mean?' he demanded.

The detective briefly related his adventure in Oxford Street. The Inspector whistled softly when he had finished.

'They certainly don't let the grass grow under their feet,' he remarked. 'What do you suppose their object was?'

'I imagine,' said Quest, smiling quietly as he helped himself to a second piece of toast, 'that they have paid me the compliment of considering that I am dangerous to their safety, and decided to take the first opportunity of putting me out of the running.'

Johnson grunted.

'Did you discover anything at Carfax's,' he asked, after a slight pause.

Quest rose to his feet and crossed to his desk, returning with the handkerchief and the green cloak room ticket. He tossed them over to the Inspector and resumed his seat at the table.

'There's no doubt whatever that Audrey Nesbitt was at Carfax's flat last night. But I think the most important clue we have got so far is the cloak room ticket. It doesn't belong to Carfax or to his manservant, Collins, so it must have been left behind by the person who entered the flat.'

'You think the girl dropped it?' enquired Johnson, as he closely examined the piece of green paper.

Quest shook his head, and for a second a peculiar smile played about the corners of his firm set mouth.

'No, I don't think the girl dropped it,' he said quietly.

The Inspector favoured him with a sharp glance.

'Do you mean there were two people then?' he asked quickly.

'Possibly,' said Quest evasively.

He rose and crossing to the mantelpiece took a cigarette from the box.

'There is a mystery surrounding Audrey Nesbitt,' he said presently, 'and I intend to get to the bottom of it.'

'I have been thinking it over, Quest,' said Johnson. 'Do you think it possible that she can be the unknown leader of the gang?'

'No, Johnson,' replied Quest decidedly. 'Carfax made the same suggestion last night, but I think it's absolutely impossible. The brain at the head of the 'Devil's Dozen' organisation is too clever to leave behind clues like that handkerchief. What the girl has got to do with it I don't know, but after I have been down to Victoria and had a look at the contents of the bag deposited by the owner of that ticket I shall go up to Bloomsbury and see if I can't persuade her to tell me all she knows.'

'Why not have her arrested,' said Johnson, 'we have plenty of evidence to arrest her on suspicion.'

'No, no,' said Quest quickly. 'It would have the effect of spoiling any chance there may be of getting her to talk.'

'All right,' grunted the Inspector. 'Have it your own way. When are you going to Victoria?'

'Immediately,' replied Quest.

'I think I'll come along with you,' said Johnson. 'I wish to goodness we could come to the end of this business,' he continued irritably, rubbing at his bristly moustache. 'We have been trying now for nearly eight months to round up the 'Devil's Dozen,' and the further we go the more tangled the affair seems to become.'

'I don't think we shall have to wait much longer,' remarked Philip Quest, as he crossed to the door of his dressing-room. 'I should like to bet that before another week has passed we shall have the whole gang — including the 'Stranger.' I won't keep you a moment, Johnson,' he added, and passed into his dressing-room.

'Now I wonder what he meant by that?' muttered Johnson to himself.

When Quest returned he had discarded his dressing-gown, and together they set off for Victoria Station.

On giving up the ticket at the cloak room Quest received in exchange a medium-sized, evidently new, leather suit-case.

The detective made known his identity to the porter in charge who handed the article over the counter.

'I want to ask you one or two questions concerning this case,' he said. 'I suppose you don't happen to remember who deposited it?'

The porter scratched his head thoughtfully.

'We get so many, sir,' he said dubiously, 'I'm afraid I couldn't say, and then it's quite possible that I wasn't on duty when it was handed in.' He glanced at the ticket. 'You see, it has been here nearly six weeks I'm afraid I can't help you at all. My mate might be able to, though,' he added, as the bright idea struck him. 'I'll call him over.'

He whistled to another man who was engaged in pasting labels on to some luggage at the far side of the office, and in answer to his summons he came up to the counter,

'Do you remember who handed this in, Harry?' he asked, indicating the suit-case.

The man looked at it for some moments and then shook his head.

'Couldn't tell you,' he declared. 'You see,' he explained, 'we get a tremendous rush here at times when the Continental trains come in, and it's almost as much as we can do to deal with the stuff.'

Quest nodded.

'I was afraid you couldn't remember,' he said, slipping half a crown into the man's palm. 'Is there anywhere quiet where we can open this case?'

'You can come round to the back, sir,' said the porter, and, followed by Johnson, Quest made his way through the little door at the side of the cloak room.

They laid the suit-case on the top of a large trunk, and Quest examined the locks. They were stronger than those usually to be found on a bag of this

143

description, but the detective didn't waste time in picking them. With the sharp blade of his penknife he cut through the leather surrounding the hasps, and in a few moments the bag was open. As he raised the lid Inspector Johnson craned eagerly forward and as he caught sight of the contents he gave vent to a gasp of amazement!

For the bag was packed to the brim with bank-notes of all denominations!

'Great Scott, Quest!' the Scotland Yard man ejaculated, 'there's a fortune there.'

The detective made no reply, but commenced searching amongst the mass of paper money.

Presently he withdrew a small, black japanned tin box. It was not locked and the detective raised the lid. It contained a wig, a false beard and moustache, a bottle of Annatto stain and a collection of grease paint, and cosmetics. Underneath was a safety razor and a new tube of shaving cream! It was evidently a complete disguise outfit.

'All prepared for a quick get-away,' murmured Quest, as he examined the box carefully. 'There should be no difficulty, Johnson, in tracing some of these notes.'

The Inspector nodded.

'I'll get on to it at once,' he replied.

Quest examined the suit-case, but there was nothing to show where it had been bought, and after a time the detective closed the lid.

'You might also try and trace the makeup box,' he suggested. 'It was supplied by a well-known firm of theatrical dealers in Wardour Street, and there's the possibility that they might remember the person who bought it.'

Inspector Johnson agreed.

'I'll take this to the Yard first,' he said indicating the suit-case,

'And set a man,' put in Quest, 'to make enquiries at some of the other stations. I shouldn't be surprised if you found a similar case at almost all of them.'

'You think they have deposited one at every station?' the Inspector enquired.

'I think it's quite possible,' replied Quest.

Johnson obtained a piece of string from the man in charge of the cloak room, and with it temporarily fastened the lid of the suit-case. They left the station together, Johnson carrying the suit-case. Outside Quest stopped.

'I'm going up to Bloomsbury now,' he said, 'to interview Audrey Nesbitt.'

'All right, Quest,' said Johnson. 'I'll drop into your office later and let you know the result of my enquiries — if there is any result,' he added, pessimistically.

Quest gripped his hand and went in search of a taxi to take him to Bloomsbury Square.

Although he scarcely liked to admit it to himself, his real reason for visiting Audrey Nesbitt's flat was the hope that by doing so he might be able to discover some reason for the continued absence of his partner.

He stopped the taxi outside the Imperial Hotel, in Southampton Row, and walked quickly across Russell Square. A few minutes later he was ringing her bell.

There was no answer to his first ring and after a little while the detective pressed the push again. Still there was no reply and Quest was forced to the conclusion that the girl was out.

However, he decided to try once more, which he did, and after waiting some time without receiving an answer to his summons he was on the point of giving it up when a woman came out.

She was a sharp-featured, elderly woman, with a face that was not so pleasant to look upon, and carried an empty shopping bag on her arm, evidently on the point of setting out to do her shopping.

'Can you tell me,' he asked politely, raising his hat, 'if Miss Audrey Nesbitt is at home?'

'How should I know,' she snapped. 'You had better go up and see for yourself. Her flat is on the second floor.'

Quest thanked her and she went on down the street while the detective ascended the stairs in search of the girl's flat. He quickly found it, for it was the door facing the landing on the second floor, and grasping the little brass knocker he gave a sharp rat-tat and waited.

There was no reply.

The girl must be out, he thought, unless she had seen him approaching the house and had decided not to answer the door.

He stooped down and listened at the letter box, but from within all was silent. He straightened up and had almost made up his mind to go away and return later when he happened to catch sight of the key-hole.

It was an ordinary lock of the Yale type, but the detective noticed that across the surface of the brass was a deep scratch which continued on into the paint work of the door itself. He bent closer. The door had evidently been forced open, for the lock was twisted almost out of its setting!

Filled with a vague sense of alarm, Philip Quest pressed his shoulder to the door. It gave way unexpectedly under his weight and swung open. The latch had apparently been shattered and the door had only been closed.

He stepped into the tiny passage, and stopped, listening intently, but there wasn't a sound. A door on the right stood open and the detective peeped in.

The room was comfortably furnished as a sitting room, neat and orderly. Over one chair was thrown the black silk coat that Audrey Nesbitt had been wearing when she arrived at Portman Square, and hanging on the back of the same chair was the girl's small black hat.

There was nothing here to interest the detective, and he went on farther. He found himself in a tiny kitchen. On the table were the remains of a meal, and by the chair were a pair of shoes, but of the girl there was no sign.

On the left of the passage was another door, this was shut. Quest went across and turned the handle and looked in. The sight that met his gaze was a startling one!

The room was a bedroom, once daintily furnished but now in the utmost disorder, most of its contents had been flung about the floor in every direction. A big wardrobe gaped open and the articles it had contained were flung carelessly in a heap on the floor, and on the bed, tightly bound hand and foot, a gag tied about her mouth, lay Audrey Nesbitt!

9

Audrey Nesbitt's Story

After recovering from his first shock of amazement, Philip Quest acted swiftly.

In two strides he was at the girl's side, and taking a penknife from his pocket, slashed through the cords that bound her and quickly removed the gag from between her lips.

She was fully dressed, a fact that Quest noticed with some surprise. Her eyes held a terrified expression as she gazed up at the detective. She had evidently received a great shock, for it was some time before she recovered herself sufficiently to be able to sit up, assisted by Quest's arm round her shoulders.

Her wrists were red and sore where the cords had bitten deeply into the soft flesh and she began mechanically to chafe these as she stared wide eyed at Quest. Twice she opened her mouth to speak, but the gag had rendered her throat dry and hard and the words would not come.

Hurrying into the little kitchen Quest returned with a glass of water, which the girl drank eagerly. It seemed to revive her, for the staring, frightened look slowly left her eyes.

'It's — it's Mr. Quest, isn't it?' she murmured huskily, pushing back the fair hair from her forehead with a trembling hand. 'I — I — didn't expect to see you.'

'I suppose not,' answered the detective gently. 'Do you feel sufficiently recovered to tell me what had happened; who bound and gagged you like that, and why?'

'I don't know,' she answered after a pause. 'The man was masked, I never saw his face.'

'What man?' asked Quest.

'The man who broke in last night,' she replied. 'I was just going to bed when I heard a noise at the front door and I went along the passage to see what it was. I had almost reached the door when it suddenly burst open, and a man came in. Before I could cry out or raise an alarm he had pressed a hand tightly over my mouth and dragged me along into this room. He was dressed in a long, dark overcoat and wore a soft hat pulled down over his eyes, and the upper part of his face was concealed by a mask of some black material. I think I must have fainted for I don't remember any more, and when I came to I was bound and as you found me. The room had been pulled to pieces, but the man in the mask was gone.'

'There was nothing about him,' asked Quest, 'which would enable you to recognise him again?'

She shook her head.

'Only that he had a beard,' she replied. 'A grey beard that covered his chin.'

Into the detective's eyes crept a little gleam.

'Do you know any reason for the attack?' asked Quest.

She was silent for some moments and it seemed to the detective as if she were seeking time in which to think out her reply.

'No,' she replied at length, almost inaudibly.

Quest looked at her steadily.

'I came to see if you would be frank with me, Miss Nesbitt,' he said. 'Will you give me an honest answer to a few questions?'

Again she paused before replying.

'What do you want to know?' she asked in a low voice.

'In the first place I want to know what connection you have with the 'Devil's Dozen'?' he questioned, fixing keen but not unkindly eyes on her face. 'And why you broke into Norman Carfax's flat last night?'

She was resting on her elbow, her strained face turned towards him, her eyes slightly narrowed, and at his question he saw her start and tremble, saw the tremendous effort she made to recover her composure.

'You talk in riddles, Mr. Quest,' she answered, in a strained voice. 'I don't know what you mean.'

A hint of hardness crept into the detective's voice as he said:

'What's the use of denying it, Miss Nesbitt. Your handkerchief was found in

Mr. Carfax's study.'

Her eyes filled with tears, but she bit her lip and choked them back.

'You're very kind, Mr. Quest,' she said in a low voice. 'Perhaps it would have been better if I had told you all at first. But — I was so worried, I didn't know which way to turn.'

She broke off and stopped for a moment, as if at a loss for words.

'I don't quite know how to begin,' she went on helplessly. 'But I think I ought to start by telling you that my name is not Nesbitt. My real name is Audrey Harlowe.'

In spite of his usual self-control, Philip Quest gave a start of surprise.

'Audrey Harlowe!' he repeated in amazement. 'Are you related then to Jefferson Harlowe?'

'I am his daughter!' she announced, 'and in admitting it I feel no shame, for I am the daughter of an innocent man.'

She paused again and Quest waited, wondering what was coming next. So this accounted for the fact of the girl's being in court on the morning of the last day of

Jefferson Harlowe's trial.

'There's no need for me to tell you that father was a member of the 'Devil's Dozen,' you know that already,' she continued, her face fixed on the wall above the detective's head. 'He admitted it during the trial, but he didn't say how he came to be associated with the terrible organisation. He was forced into it, Mr. Quest' — she leaned towards Quest as she spoke — 'forced into it against his will!

'At one time, years ago, father was employed as cashier in the London and Northern Bank, and in order to meet a pressing debt he foolishly forged a cheque in the name of one of the customers of the bank. The forgery was never discovered, and later father repaid every penny of the money that he had obtained by this means.

'I suppose that in the eyes of the law he was guilty of a crime, but morally he had made reparation and believed that the incident was done with. But, by some means or other the knowledge and proofs of this act of father's came into the hands of the most pitiless and inhuman scoundrel who ever lived.'

Her eyes blazed for a moment and her little hands gripped the folds of the coverlet, and the detective was astounded at the expression of concentrated hate which he saw in her face. It seemed impossible to believe that such a frail-looking girl could be capable of so strong an emotion.

'I am referring to the 'Stranger',' she went on when she had sufficiently recovered herself to speak again. 'He wrote to father one day and offered him the alternative of either joining the 'Devil's Dozen' or having the story of the forgery made public.

'Of course you understand, Mr. Quest, I knew nothing of this at the time, and it was not until a long while after that I learnt the full facts. I don't think at first father was fully aware of the true nature of the organisation of which he had become a part, but when the truth became apparent to him, he took me into his confidence and told me the whole story, which I have told briefly to you. He was convinced that owing to his association with the 'Devil's Dozen' some kind of disaster would, sooner or later, overtake him.

'His one thought was for me and the fear that if anything of a discreditable nature had happened I should become mixed up in it. I think at the time he feared arrest and was worried lest I should be pointed out as the daughter of a felon.

'It was then that he insisted that I should change my name to Nesbitt — (it was my mother's maiden name) — and live apart from him in this flat. We had very few friends and as far as the 'Stranger' was concerned he did not even know that father possessed a daughter, and father was most particular that our relationship should be kept a secret. I refused at first, but my refusal seemed to worry him and caused him so much unhappiness that eventually I consented.

'It was some time after this that quite by accident I met Robert Deering. I had been in the employ of Sir Lionel Trevor for about eighteen months and one evening I had to execute a commission for him that took me to Lambeth. You know what some of the streets are like round there, Mr. Quest, and I did not know the district at all. After completing my business I went down a side street which I thought was a short cut to the Tube. I was in rather a hurry because I had an — an appointment' — she reddened and stopped for a moment in confusion. 'The street proved to be a cul-de-sac,' she continued presently, 'and I turned to retrace my steps. There were two rough-looking men who had been standing at the end and as I passed them they started to follow me. They rapidly overtook me and I grew frightened. It was evident that they had been drinking and when they drew level with me their behaviour became insulting.

'I started to run, hoping to get to the main road where there were people about, but one of them gripped me by the arm and stopped me.

'I screamed and at that moment a young man came running up. He demanded to know what had happened, and told the men to clear off, but they refused and blows were struck. How it would have ended I don't know but a policeman arrived and the two men were taken into custody.

'My rescuer had twisted his ankle and could hardly walk, but he said that it was nothing and that he only lived round the corner. But I could see that he was in great pain, and I could scarcely let him go after what he had done for me so I insisted on helping him as far as his door.

'He was very poorly dressed and looked ill, and I persuaded him to tell me his name with the intention of trying to repay him in some way for the service he had rendered me. He told me his name was Deering, and shortly after we arrived at the top of the street in which he lived. He wouldn't let me come any farther but told me his number and then showed me the quickest way to the Tube Station.

'The following day I called at his house to see how his ankle was getting on. It was the least I could do, seeing that he was injured in trying to save me from an unpleasant situation. It was a dreadful house in which he lived, miserable and almost falling to pieces, and he looked to me as if he was half starved. I asked him if I could help him in any way, but he only shook his head and refused to allow me to do anything for him.

'I don't know what led the conversation round that way, but I happened to mention that I was secretary to Sir Lionel Trevor. When he heard the name he became greatly agitated and started to ask me questions concerning Sir Lionel. Naturally I didn't answer them. I could scarcely speak about my employer to a stranger and he seemed to realise this, for on seeing my reluctance he refrained from questioning me further and shortly after I left.'

She stopped and reaching out her hand for the glass of water Quest had placed on the table by the bedside, drank a little.

The detective was listening, for he was intensely interested in the girl's story.

'I had almost forgotten the incident,' she continued, 'when about a week later a parcel arrived for me at Sir Lionel's house.

I couldn't imagine who it could be from, but on opening it I discovered that it contained an old black japanned deed box, and a note. The box was tied round with string and heavily sealed, and the note was from Robert Deering. As near as I can remember it merely asked me to keep the box until under any circumstances I should hear of the sender's death. In which case I was to deliver it personally to Sir Lionel Trevor. In the meantime I was to say nothing to him whatever about having received it.

'It seemed to me a peculiar request, but it was very little trouble, and I decided to accede to Deering's request. I brought the box home to this flat and forgot all about it, but about ten days after it was brought back to my mind by reading an account of Robert Deering's death in the paper.

'I had put the box on the top shelf of that cupboard' — she pointed to the wardrobe in the corner — 'but when I went to look for it to give to Sir Lionel it was gone. Who had taken it or when I hadn't the least idea.

'I meant to mention the matter to Sir Lionel, but just at that time my father was arrested for the murder of Charles Benson, and the terrible shock drove everything else out of my mind. I knew that there had been a terrible mistake, and that he was innocent, and I made up my mind to obtain proof.

'On the few occasions when I have met father since we have been living apart we had often speculated as to the possible identity of the 'Stranger' and father once showed me a typewritten letter of instructions which he received from the leader of the 'Devil's Dozen.' I had forgotten to give it back to him, and I don't know why, but for some reason I kept it.

'There was a slight peculiarity in some of the letters which I had noticed, and then one day, among Sir Lionel's correspondence, I came across a letter which possessed the same defects in the type. It was a slight clue, but it set me on the track of the 'Stranger.'

'I was certain that if I could find this mysterious person I should be able to obtain the proofs of father's innocence. It would have been useless my going to the police, for I was convinced that they would merely have laughed at me if I had mentioned the person against whom my suspicions were directed, and so I went to work on my own.

'Since then I have been working night and day to prove to the world that my father is innocent of the terrible crime for which he has been convicted and sentenced. The truth cannot remain hidden for ever and I feel that I am already nearing victory.'

Her eyes were shining now, and as Philip Quest saw the splendid character of the girl expressed in her face he was conscious of a feeling of intense admiration for her plucky fighting spirit.

'Your determination to find proofs of your father's innocence is a very laudable one,' he said sincerely, 'but your actions have laid you open to very grave suspicion, besides which it is a task that is above your powers to accomplish apart

163

from the terrible risk that you ran in attempting it. Had the 'Stranger' been aware of what you were doing there is not the slightest doubt that you wouldn't be alive at this moment. I myself believe that your father is guiltless of the crime of which he has been accused, and I have already made a vow to do all in my power to prove his innocence.'

'Thank you for saying that, Mr. Quest,' she murmured gratefully, her eyes wet with unshed tears. 'If I had only come to you in the first place . . . but I never dreamed.'

'Of course you didn't,' said Quest gently. 'But it is not too late now, Miss Nesbitt. I want you to take me entirely into your confidence and tell me the name of the person you suspect being the 'Stranger.''

She hesitated for a moment and then leaning forwards whispered a name.

Philip Quest started as he heard it, for her suspicions coincided with his own.

For a long time they remained in earnest conversation, and when the detective took his departure he made his way back to his rooms with a very grave and thoughtful expression upon his clear cut features, for to Philip Quest the secret of the 'Stranger' was a secret no longer!

10

The Disused Factory

Richard Lester recovered consciousness to find himself in pitch darkness. His head throbbed violently, and his whole body felt stiff and sore.

For a long time he lay in a half-dazed condition, striving to clear the mist from his brain and to recollect what had happened.

As he began to recover the full use of his senses he discovered that the darkness was due to the fact that his head had been wrapped tightly in some opaque material, the ends of which had been tied beneath his chin.

He attempted to raise his hand to discover what this was, but found that it was impossible, his hands had been securely tied to his sides, and investigating further he found that this also applied to his ankles.

His throat felt dry, and in attempting to moisten his lips with his tongue he discovered that a gag had been forced into his mouth. After making one or two attempts and finding that it was impossible to move his limbs so much as an inch he lay still.

He stifled a groan, the pain in his head was acute, and the slightest movement was agony and made him feel sick and dizzy. Presently he became aware of a curious vibration that seemed to be going on all the time, and for which, at first, he could not account. It was a rhythmic, humming noise, and was accompanied by a movement that shook his whole body. He began to try and seek some cause for this movement. He appeared to be lying on something soft and springy which was continually bumping up and down, and presently it was borne to his mind that he must be in some sort of vehicle.

He felt about with the tips of his fingers and presently his sense of touch informed him that he was lying on some kind of cushion, the material of which appeared to be something like a corded velvet.

This fact, in conjunction with the faint humming noise and the bumping led Lester to come to the conclusion that he was in a car. He tried to wriggle his head free of the enveloping folds of cloth in which it had been wrapped, but it caused him so much pain that he was forced to give up the attempt.

By the motion of the car it seemed to be travelling at a considerable speed, and he began to conjecture as to its possible destination.

The whole thing had come back to him now in the street off Russell Square, and the figure that had sprung at him out of the mist.

Was it the grey bearded man who had followed Audrey Nesbitt and Jack Archer who had struck him down? In the faint glimpse that he had caught of his assailant before the blow had rendered him unconscious he had seemed vaguely familiar, but Lester could not be certain if he was the same man. The whole thing had happened so quickly that he had not had time to catch more than a fleeting shadow of his attacker.

How long he had been in the car he had no idea. They might have been travelling for a considerable time while he had lain unconscious.

If he could only get his head free from that infernal cloth, he thought, he might be able to discover where he was and perhaps glean some idea from his surroundings of the direction in which he was being taken.

That he was in the power of the 'Devil's Dozen' he hadn't a doubt, and the question that remained was, what did they intend doing with him? That a particularly unpleasant time lay in front of him he was certain. He had no delusions concerning the gang and he knew that unless he could manage to elude them in some way and make his escape he would be lucky if he got off with his life.

There was no cessation in the speed at which the machine was travelling, and it ran on and on while the time dragged slowly by. Some time after the road appeared to alter its character for the car no longer ran as smoothly as it had done and Lester concluded, by the bumpy nature of the surface over which they were passing, that they were now travelling on a road which was little used. There was a violent jerk and he was nearly thrown off his seat as suddenly the car ran sharply to the right. It continued on but in a little while he felt the speed slacken, and presently it slowed down to scarcely more than a crawl, and shortly after came to a stop.

There was the sound of a click, followed almost immediately by the slamming of a door, and Lester heard stumbling footsteps receding in the distance. Evidently the man who had been driving had left the car and gone off somewhere, and Lester wondered what was going to happen next. By the sound of the footsteps there appeared to have been only one man in the car besides himself.

Presently he heard the sound of voices; they were faint at first but gradually drew nearer, and Lester was able to distinguish the tones of two men. So the driver had gone to fetch a companion.

'What are you going to do with him?' asked a voice, and the young man felt a draught of cold air as the door beside his head was jerked open.

'Put him upstairs,' came the reply. 'You'd better help me carry him, Grogan.'

Lester felt himself being lifted out of the car. He relaxed his muscles and allowed his body to remain limp in order to allow his captors into imagining that he had not yet recovered his senses, by doing so he hoped to pick up some information concerning his whereabouts, but he was destined to be disappointed, they were careful to keep the cloth wrapped round his head.

For about a hundred yards they carried him stumbling, and cursing over the roughness of the ground, and then Lester heard the sound of their footfalls alter as they struck on wood. By the hollowness of the sound he concluded that they had entered a building.

'He's no light weight,' panted the voice that had spoken first.

'Well, we haven't much farther to carry him,' replied his companion, 'only to the top of these stairs.'

Lester felt himself being carried up a short flight of stairs. At the top his captors paused, breathing hard.

'You've got the key, Bennet,' said the man who had complained of his weight, 'you'd better unlock the door.'

They deposited Lester none too lightly on the floor and he heard the sound of a key being inserted in a lock.

'He'll be all right here,' said the man who had been addressed as Bennet, as they picked him up and carried him a short distance farther in.

'How long is he going to stop here?' asked the other man.

'I don't know,' was the reply. 'The only order I got was to bring him here, and I don't know anything else.'

Lester felt himself laid down on some hard boards, heard the door slam and the click of the lock as it was fastened after them, and then the sound of their footsteps as they descended the stairs.

He lay for a moment motionless, and then presently began to test the cords which bound his wrists. To his intense satisfaction he found that these had become slightly loosened during the journey from the car, and he began to work on them in the hope of being able to free his hands.

At last, after what seemed a considerable time but in reality could not have been more than fifteen or twenty minutes, he felt one of the cords give a little. He redoubled his efforts and soon was rewarded by being able to drag one hand free. His wrists were raw and painful but there was no time to heed that. With his free hand he tore the cloth from about his head, but even then he could not see much for the place was in complete darkness.

His nimble fingers set to work on the remaining knots, and in a few moments the other hand was free. It took him less than five minutes to move the gag from between his lips and untie the cords which bound his ankles. The exertion, however, aggravated the pain in his head, and the throbbing was so great that for a moment he felt his senses swim and he almost lost consciousness again. He lay still for a while with his eyes closed and in a few minutes had recovered sufficiently to give himself the treatment which Philip Quest had taught him.

He sat up and dropping his chin on his breast placed his two open hands behind his neck, the finger tips pressing hard. Then he slowly raised his head, bringing his fingers down over the jugular vein. It was agony while it lasted, but after it had been three times repeated he felt considerably better, and his head was comparatively clear.

Then Lester began to take an interest in his surroundings. He felt in his pocket and found that his captors had not removed his matches, and producing the box he struck one and looked about him. By its feeble light he was able to take a swift glance at the place in which he had been confined.

It was a long, low room, the windows of which had apparently been boarded up, the walls appeared to be of concrete and scattered about the floor were pieces of machinery. The whole place was full of rubbish of all sorts and the floor was covered with a thick layer of dust.

The match went out and he had to strike another before he could continue his examination. Across the ceiling ran a line of broken shafting and in one corner, fastened to a concrete base, were the remains of some kind of engine. The place looked as though at one time it had been a factory. It was plain, however, that it had not been in use for some time for everything about the place spelt decay and neglect.

As his second match burnt down to his fingers he rose and tiptoed over to the door, here he struck his third match. The door was a heavy one and it did not require much examination on his part for him to come to the conclusion that it was impossible for him to escape by that means.

He turned his attention to the windows. They had apparently been used more as a means of ventilation than of admitting light, and he saw that even if they had not been boarded up they were much too small to have allowed anyone to pass through.

Between the windows he came upon a large electric switch. He pulled it down, hoping that it controlled the light, but apparently it did not, or else the current was off, for nothing happened. Running to and from the switch was a thick, heavy insulated cable, and following it with his eyes he saw that one end finished beside the broken piece of machinery, that looked to him like some form of motor. Instantly the use of the cable flashed to his mind. It had been the means of supplying power to the machinery in the corner.

He paused in his investigations and listened. The murmur of voices had suddenly come to his ears from below. The floor was thick and he came to the conclusion that there must be some connection between the room he was in and the place below, otherwise he could not have heard the sound so clearly. He began to search about and soon discovered the reason. Projecting close to the floor by the side of a dilapidated bench which ran the full length of the wall under the boarded windows was the broken end of a speaking tube.

Lester bent down and applied his ear to the opening and instantly the voices became more clearly audible. The men were apparently engaged in discussing him, for he heard one of them say:

'We can't keep him here indefinitely, it's too risky.'

'We've got to wait and see what the Boss has to say,' replied the other. 'The only order I've got so far is to bring him here, what's got to happen to him after that I don't know. I'm waiting to hear.'

The voices sank to a whisper after that, and Lester could not distinguish anything further.

Evidently his fate depended on the Boss, whoever he was, and he thought that it was fairly obvious that if he was in the power of the 'Devil's Dozen' the Boss referred to must be the 'Stranger.' He listened again at the tube and presently he heard a chair scrape as one of the men rose.

'I shan't be long,' and it was Bennet who spoke. 'He said he would let me know at five o'clock, and it's just on that now.'

Lester heard the man's footsteps crossing the floor.

The five o'clock, he concluded, could only be five o'clock in the morning, for it must have been somewhere round about half past ten when he had been attacked off Russell Square.

Bennet was gone about half an hour, and then Lester heard his footsteps returning.

'Well, what have we got to do with him?' asked the other, as he came back.

There was a pause, and then:

'The 'Stranger' says he's got to die!' came the reply in a low voice.

11

A Dash for Liberty

Richard Lester, kneeling on the floor by the speaking tube, heard the words clearly, and his heart went cold within him at the matter of fact way in which the man spoke.

'What does he want him killed for?' asked the voice of Grogan.

'How should I know,' snarled Bennet, irritably. 'If the Boss says he's got to die, he's got to die, and that's that. Anyhow, he'll be safer out of the way.'

'I don't like it,' replied the other uneasily. 'If anything happens to him Quest will — '

'Oh, shut up,' broke in his companion roughly. 'What's the matter with you. You're getting squeamish all of a sudden, aren't you? You needn't worry your head about Quest, the 'Stranger' will settle him. He's got more brains than a thousand Philip Quests!'

Grogan muttered something in a voice too low for Lester to catch, and a long silence followed.

Then Lester rose from beside the speaking tube and started to think quickly.

There was no knowing how soon they would prepare to carry out their instructions and come in search of him to obey the 'Stranger's' command. He had no intention of sitting idly by and waiting to be done to death, but if he was going to do anything it had to be done quickly.

He forced his brain to work at express speed. He was in a tight corner and somehow he was going to get out of it. But the question was how?

He struck another of his matches and took a further survey of the room in which he was imprisoned. It was hopeless to think of escaping by the door, it was too solid and would require a battering ram or a dose of gunpowder to shift, and Lester was not possessed of either, and even if he had been the resulting noise would only tend to bring the men downstairs up at a run. The windows, too, were, impossible and a child could not have got through.

The match went out, leaving him in the dark again. There must be some way out, thought the young man, and his alert brain worked busily to find a solution to the problem before him.

The sound of voices downstairs had ceased entirely, and he wondered what the two men were up to, and with a grim smile about his mouth the thought came to him that they were in all probability planning the means by which he was to die.

It seemed a hopeless situation, for he could think of no way by which it was possible to escape from his prison.

It was the end, and he had to face it like a rat in a trap. And then suddenly, in a flash, an inspiration came to him. He remembered the power cable that ran through the switch to the dismantled motor in the corner of the room.

Stooping down he noiselessly removed his shoes so that the sound of his movements would not be heard by the

181

men he believed were still in the room below. Moving stealthily across the floor and taking care to test each board before putting his weight on it, lest a creak should warn them that he was free, Lester approached that side of the wall in which were two narrow windows. Reaching up carefully he groped about with his hands in the dark and presently found what he was seeking — the electric cable. He gripped it in his strong fingers and pulled steadily. Under his weight the supporting insulator broke loose, and by great good luck, fell upon a heap of rubbish and made no sound.

The cable was now free from the wall and for the next quarter of an hour he worked feverishly, unwrapping the insulation from the wires of one end of the cable and pulling the copper strands free. It was difficult work, for he had to do it in the dark, as it was impossible to hold a match and carry out his task at the same time.

His hands were bleeding and his nails broken, but after a quarter of an hour's work he had managed to fray out the ends of the cable.

He had hardly finished before he heard the sound of a movement in the room below, and presently, the noise of a stealthy footstep on the stairs.

Only one thing now bothered Lester — was the current turned on at the main. He had not dared to take the risk of testing it for fear of causing a short circuit and so ruining all chances of his plan being a success. It had been difficult enough as it was to keep the two frayed ends of the cable from coming in contact with each other.

The sound of the foot-fall came nearer, and grasping the thick wire, Lester tiptoed over to the door and waited. There came a faint whisper from outside, followed by the noise of the key in the lock.

To Richard Lester, waiting with muscles, tensed and every nerve in his body strained, it seemed an eternity before the door opened.

A figure entered and a bright ray of light flashed out as the man switched on an electric torch. He advanced two paces and then Lester acted.

He stepped swiftly forward and thrust the two brush-like ends of the wire into the man's face. He gave a yell of pain as the current passed through his body, which ended in a gasping sob as he fell backward and dropped to the floor.

'Hello! Grogan,' cried the voice of Bennet from half way up the stairs. 'What the deuce is the matter?'

Lester heard him come up the rest of the flight of stairs at a run, his feet clattering loudly on the bare boards.

He had only taken one step into the room when the frayed wire struck him. He gave vent to a howling cry of surprise, stood motionless for a moment, and then fell forward over the body of the other man.

Lester didn't wait any longer. Dropping the cable and jumping over the groaning bodies of the two men he leaped down the stairs. As he reached the bottom he glanced into the room below. It had evidently been the office of the factory, and was empty, but on the old rickety table lay an automatic pistol. Running in he picked up the weapon. It would be useful, he thought, in case there were any more of the gang about that he had not seen.

The sound of movements from upstairs warned him that Bennet and Grogan were recovering from the electric shock. As he came out of the door of the office he heard a shout, and glancing up quickly, saw Bennet at the head of the stairs.

The man caught sight of him at the same moment. Lester raised the pistol and pressed the trigger, but there was only a sharp click — the magazine was empty!

Bennet was coming down the stairs in pursuit, calling loudly to the other, and Lester fled along the bare factory hall, through a door, and out into the open.

He tried to reach the road which appeared to him to be separated by only a line of bushes, but here he blundered. The bushes concealed a fence of thickly interlaced barbed wire, which Lester did not discover until he was almost upon it!

He looked about swiftly, hoping to find a break in the wire but there was none! He was caught in a trap!

Bennet and Grogan were racing towards him now, and Lester doubled back and flew in the direction of some sheds which stood by the side of the main building. The ground was rough and uneven and covered with sharp stones, and running in his stockinged feet was painful. His progress in consequence was necessarily slow and his pursuers were gaining on him.

Lester gave a hurried glance back over his shoulder as he raced along. Bennet had drawn a pistol from his pocket and as he looked the man fired and the bullet whined angrily past his ears.

The situation was becoming desperate. At such short range it was scarcely possible that they could miss him!

'Don't shoot, you fool,' shouted Grogan, 'we've got him now. There's no exit that way, and the noise of the shots might bring someone along to see what's the matter!'

Bennet grunted a reply. He was leading and Lester could hear his breath as it came in great panting gasps from his throat. He reached the sheds and found that they were built against a high brick wall!

One look assured him that there was no escape that way, and the next moment the men were on him. Bennet leaped on him, grasping and tearing with open hands.

'I'll fix you, you devil!' he cried, his eyes glaring. 'You shall try a dose of electric shock yourself.'

He drove his fist in Lester's face, but the younger man twisted his head to one side and the blow struck the brickwork of the shed against which he was standing. The man started back with a howl of pain, the blood pouring from his grazed knuckles. Yelling a string of curses he made another rush at Lester, but he stepped forward and met him half way, striking out scientifically. His blow landed straight and clean on Bennet's jaw, and the man collapsed.

He swung round in time to ward off Grogan who had sprung at him from behind, but he was too late. The man's groping fingers found and gripped his throat, and try as he would Lester could not break that strangle hold.

There came a booming roar in his ears and flashes and splashes of red danced before his eyes . . . The blood hammered madly in his brain . . . He could feel his senses reeling . . .

'Let him go and put up your hands!' cried a sharp voice suddenly, and Lester felt himself released.

He staggered and leaned against the shed wall for support, panting.

Grogan was standing stupidly with his hands raised above his head.

Lester looked at his rescuer and gave a cry of amazement, for the man who was holding up Grogan with a revolver was Charles Benson's late secretary, Jack Archer!

12

The Letter from Oxford

When Philip Quest reached his chambers in the City he discovered to his surprise and relief that Lester had returned during his absence.

His partner was perched on a corner of the table in the consulting-room talking to Inspector Johnson and a young man whom Quest recognised immediately. Lester looked round with a cheery grin as the detective entered.

'Hello!' he cried. 'I'm glad you've come, I've got lots to tell you. You know Mr. Archer, don't you?' he nodded in the direction of the young man. 'I shouldn't be here now if it hadn't been for him.'

Quest crossed over and took the hand that Archer extended to him.

'I was getting quite anxious about you,' he said turning to Lester. 'What happened to you. Tell me all about it.'

He seated himself in a chair by the side of the fireplace, and Lester launched forth into a vivid account of his adventures of the previous night while the detective listened gravely.

'I was never more surprised in my life,' Lester concluded as he reached the point in his narrative where Jack Archer had appeared. 'It was jolly lucky for me you were there, but you were the last person I expected to see.'

'It was quite by accident I was there,' said Archer with a smile. 'If I hadn't happened to be near Russell Square when that chap hit you over the head I should have known nothing about it.'

'What were you doing in Russell Square?' asked Philip Quest quickly.

Jack Archer looked confused for a moment and his face reddened slightly.

'Well — er — ' he stammered. 'I was — er — ' His voice trailed away into silence.

Quest smiled.

'You can be quite frank with me, Mr. Archer,' he said. 'I have only just left Miss Nesbitt and she has taken me entirely into her confidence, so you need have no hesitation in speaking out.'

Archer looked relieved and Inspector Johnson looked sharply at Quest.

'Have you learned anything fresh, Quest?' he interjected.

The detective nodded.

'Quite a lot, Johnson,' he replied. 'In fact I think we are nearing the end. Just a little longer and I shall have the 'Stranger' like that.' He closed his hand suddenly and his knuckles stood out white with the force of the grip.

'You probably know then, Mr. Quest,' said Archer, 'that I am engaged to Miss Nesbitt, and I suppose you also know that her real name is Harlowe and that she is the daughter of the man who was found guilty of the murder of Benson.'

Quest replied in the affirmative, and Johnson and Lester looked their astonishment.

'I also know,' the detective added, 'that for a long time she has been working to try and find proofs of her father's innocence.'

Jack Archer nodded.

'That was partly the reason that took me to Russell Square,' he said. 'Audrey and I had discussed the matter on several occasions and I tried to persuade her to tell the police all she suspected and drop her foolish idea of trying to secure proofs by herself. But she can be very obstinate when she likes and she wouldn't listen to me. Last night I met her at Piccadilly Tube Station, and we went into the Corner House in Coventry Street to talk.'

'I know,' interrupted Lester with a chuckle. 'I followed you.'

'Great Scott! I didn't know that,' replied Archer. 'I knew somebody was following us, but it was a man with a grey beard and — '

'That wasn't me,' said Lester. 'That was the other man. I believe he was the one who biffed me over the head.'

'It wasn't,' said Archer. 'I saw the one who knocked you out, and it wasn't the man with the beard, it was one of the men who were arrested at the factory at Horsham.'

'Who arrested them?' asked Quest in surprise.

'The local police,' grunted Johnson, rubbing fiercely at his moustache. 'And there's a bit of a mystery concerning that, Quest. I've been on the phone to the Inspector in charge at Horsham and he says that early this morning he received a phone message stating that a murder had been committed at Mills' old bottle factory. The informer refused all information regarding himself, and the call was put through from a public call office in London. It's a repetition of what happened in the Benson case.'

'And was done for the same reason,' murmured Quest thoughtfully, 'by the same man.

'I'd like to know what the idea is,' grunted Johnson. 'It seems mad to me.'

'It is anything but mad, but the idea is a simple one,' said Quest.

Inspector Johnson opened his mouth to put another question but the detective broke in before he could put it into words.

'Go on with what you were saying, Archer,' he said, turning to that young man. 'I am anxious to know how you came to be at hand to rescue my partner so opportunely.'

'Where had I got to?' said Jack Archer thoughtfully. 'Oh, I know. Well, we went into the Corner House and as usual started discussing the 'Devil's Dozen' and the Benson murder: Audrey was very excited and said she had a scheme which would prove conclusively her father's innocence. She wouldn't tell me what it was, but I somehow got the impression that it was going to lead her into considerable danger. I argued again and again to try and get her to give up the whole idea but she wouldn't hear of it. She never told me who she suspected of being responsible for her father's horrible position though she did tell me the story of how he had been forced into joining the 'Devil's Dozen.' However, all my arguments were, as usual, in vain and I could see that whatever it was she had made up her mind to do she would carry it through, and nothing would dissuade her.

'She left me shortly after, saying that she was going home. Her words and her whole manner had worried me considerably and I determined to follow her. I don't know why I did but I had a vague feeling that she was running into danger. This feeling became strengthened when I became certain that Audrey was being followed. Three times I had seen a grey-bearded man, once when I met her outside the Tube, again in the tea-shop, and after I left her I saw him enter a taxi and follow the bus she was on.'

'That's why I lost sight of him then,' said Lester. 'I never thought he'd take a taxi, and when he didn't board the bus I concluded he'd given up the chase.'

'He probably recognised you,' put in Quest, 'and thinking you'd spotted him decided not to risk the bus again. Go on, Archer.'

'I followed Audrey home,' continued Jack Archer, 'and saw her go in. I began to feel rather a fool, for after all it looked as though she had merely gone home to go to bed. I didn't go near the house because I was afraid she might see me and get annoyed if she thought I'd followed her after saying I was going home. I began walking up and down on the other side of Russell Square trying to make up my mind whether I'd go or not when suddenly I saw the man with the grey beard again.

'A limousine had entered the square and he was standing talking to another man by the side of it. It had drawn up near the corner of the street in which Audrey lived. He only stayed for about two minutes, however, and then walked away at a tremendous pace towards Southampton Row. I had just made up my mind to follow him to find out what his game was when I saw the man he had been talking to leave the car and go off down the street in which Audrey lived.

'I began to get afraid that some mischief was afoot, and decided to remain and see what was happening. I hadn't long to wait, for presently the man returned carrying something in his arms. I didn't know it at the time, but it must have been you!' He addressed this remark to Lester.

'The man bundled his burden into the car, and got into the back himself. He was inside some time and then he re-appeared and climbing into the driving seat started the engine. As the car moved off I made up my mind, and, running after it, succeeded in hopping on the luggage grid at the back, before it had gathered speed. I didn't know who it was who had been put in that car but I was determined to find out.'

'It's a good thing for me you were,' said Lester feelingly.

'It was very dark and I hadn't the faintest idea where we were going,' continued Archer, 'and it was anything but comfortable on that grid. I'm still sore even now,' he grinned. 'Presently we got right out in the country and were going at a good speed. After we had been going for about two hours the car suddenly veered to the right. I wasn't expecting anything like that to happen and the shock threw me off and I landed in the road.

'I must have hit my head for I don't remember anything more for some time, and dawn was breaking when I came to myself.

'I could see that the car had gone down a narrow cart track leading between some high hedges, and I decided to follow. It seemed to be miles before I saw anything but hedges, but suddenly I came in sight of two gates. They were ajar and peeping in I saw the car standing in a dirty courtyard. At the same moment I heard a frightful shindy going on inside.'

Lester grinned.

'That was when I was trying a few experiments in electricity,' he remarked.

'I pushed open the gate and saw a door opposite that was also open. As I looked in two men came flying down the stairs and went racing along a passage to another door at the far end. One of them dropped his pistol in his hurry, and after they had gone I picked it up and followed along the passage, and I was just in time to stop that big brute throttling you,' he concluded.

Philip Quest had been listening intently while Jack Archer was speaking.

'I can never thank you enough for what you did,' was all he said, but there was a world of sincerity in his voice. Then he turned to Detective-Inspector Johnson.

'I want you to put a couple of plain-clothes men to watch Miss Nesbitt night and day,' he said gravely.

Jack Archer looked at him suspiciously.

'But I thought you said she had told you everything?' he cried. 'Surely you don't still suspect — '

'No, no,' said Quest. 'It's not that. It's her safety I'm thinking of, for during the next few days Audrey Nesbitt will be in danger — terrible danger!'

'What do you mean, Quest?' asked Johnson. 'Who is she in danger from?'

'I haven't time for explanations now, Johnson,' said the detective, as he rose to his feet. 'There's a lot to be done during the next twenty-four hours, but you know me sufficiently well to be sure that I wouldn't suggest having her watched without good cause.'

Johnson shrugged his shoulders resignedly; he was used to Quest's little ways and he knew that as soon as the detective thought that the time was ripe he would divulge all he knew. It was a habit of Philip Quest's that he never talked until he was in possession of solid facts to back up his theories, and until he was in a position to prove everything he remained silent.

'All right, Quest,' he growled, 'I'll do as you say.'

Philip Quest clapped him on the shoulder.

'I won't keep you in the dark a moment longer than I can help,' he said, and the Inspector grunted.

'Have you any objection, Mr. Quest,' said Jack Archer, 'to my going round to see Audrey?'

'Not the slightest, my dear fellow,' replied the detective. 'In fact I think it an excellent idea.' He glanced at the clock. 'I must go out now,' he continued. 'I've got one or two enquiries to make. By the way, Johnson, can you find me a good photograph of Benson, a recent one?'

The Inspector thought for a moment.

'I think there's one at the Yard,' he answered after a pause.

'I'll walk as far with you,' said Quest crossing to the door.

'Isn't there anything I can do?' asked Lester.

The detective paused with his hand on the handle.

'I think you've had enough excitement for the time being,' he said with a smile, and then, seeing the disappointment on his young partner's face added: 'I think I shall have a job for you later, but not at the moment,' and Lester's face brightened.

On the way to Scotland Yard Philip Quest related to Johnson part of his interview with Audrey Nesbitt, although much of it he refrained from mentioning.

The Inspector listened attentively.

'So the box was sent to the girl to give to Sir Lionel,' he remarked when Quest had finished. 'I wonder why Deering was so anxious for it to be delivered to Trevor after his death?'

'That's one of the little mysteries that still remain to be cleared up,' replied the detective. 'The greatest mystery of all is what the box can contain that makes it of so much value to the 'Stranger,' and who took it from the girl's flat after she had taken it home.'

'It's a horrible tangle, Quest,' declared

Johnson, his forehead wrinkling under his hard bowler hat. 'It beats me, I don't mind telling you.'

'It was obviously not the 'Stranger' who stole the box,' said Quest thoughtfully, 'for he is still searching for it. So who could it have been? It must have been someone who knew it was in the girl's possession.'

'Do you think Archer could have had anything to do with it?' asked Johnson. 'He is the most likely person to have known that it was at her flat.'

Philip Quest shook his head.

'He would have had no motive,' he replied. 'No, Johnson, it must have been someone who knew Deering, and knew the contents of the box as well, and — ' He broke off and for some time relapsed into silence.

'I wonder,' he murmured presently below his breath, and Johnson gave him a quick, side-long glance. 'That box has got to be found,' continued the detective, 'as soon as we've got that the case is complete.'

'Except for discovering the identity of

the 'Stranger',' said Johnson.

'I know that already,' answered Philip Quest simply.

Inspector Johnson stopped dead and stared at him as though doubting the evidence of his own ears.

'What!' he shouted. 'You know who the 'Stranger' is?'

Quest nodded.

'Then why in Heaven's name don't we arrest him?'

'Because if we arrest him now,' said Quest, 'he would only slip through our fingers. We have got no absolute proof yet.'

'Who is he?' demanded Johnson.

'I'd rather not say anything at the moment, Johnson,' said the detective. 'As soon as I have got proof to back up my statement you shall know all about it.'

Detective-Inspector Johnson snorted and tugged at his moustache. He was inclined to be annoyed, and for the rest of the walk a silence fell between them.

Reaching Scotland Yard they ascended the stairs to Johnson's office.

'Wait a minute, Quest,' said the

Inspector, 'and I'll see if I can get that photograph for you.'

He was just crossing to the door when a sergeant entered.

'I've been looking for you, sir,' said the sergeant to Johnson.

'What do you want?' snapped the Inspector irritably.

'We've found two more of those cases, sir,' the man continued, 'one at Euston, and one at Charing Cross. They are all exactly alike.'

'Bring 'em up here,' ordered Johnson, 'I'll have a look at 'em.'

'We've also traced some of the notes,' the sergeant continued.

Johnson looked at him eagerly.

'Yes?' he enquired.

'Most of the numbers of the notes in the first case correspond with those of the notes stolen in connection with the Benson murder,' the man answered.

'You're sure of that?' asked Quest.

'Yes,' replied the sergeant. 'They have all been compared with the list issued by the bank from which Benson drew the money. I'll send the other bags up,' he added, and withdrew.

'That rather helps to prove Harlowe's story,' said Quest.

'I don't agree with you,' replied Johnson. 'You forget that the cloak room ticket was found in Carfax's flat. We know that the girl was there when it was burgled and she could easily have dropped it — and she's Jefferson Harlowe's daughter,' he added significantly.

'And you imagine that it was Harlowe who prepared those cases?' asked Quest, 'and that Audrey Nesbitt knew about it?'

'I do!' declared the Inspector.

'But he wouldn't have had time,' argued Quest. 'He was arrested immediately after the robbery in Benson's office.'

'His daughter would have had plenty of time, though,' replied Johnson.

Quest laughed.

'Nonsense, Johnson,' he said. 'I've told you that she has been spending all her time trying to prove her father's innocence. She would hardly do that if she knew her father was guilty.'

'You've only got her word for that,'

persisted the Inspector. 'And it may only be a blind.'

Philip Quest shrugged his shoulders.

'Oh, well, we shall see,' he answered. 'But I assure you you're wrong.'

A constable arrived with the two suitcases that had been found at Euston and Charing Cross. They were exactly the same as the one they had discovered at Victoria, and the contents similar in every particular.

'I don't think there is much to be learned from these,' said Quest, when he and Johnson had examined them. 'If you will give me that photograph, I'll be getting off.'

Johnson gave some instructions to the constable who hurried away, and after a short interval returned with an envelope which the Inspector handed to Quest.

'Where are you going now?' he asked.

'I'm going first to Lambeth,' answered the detective, 'and after that I've one or two enquiries to make in the City, and then I want to have a few words with the two men who were arrested at Horsham.'

He said good-bye to Johnson and hurried away.

It was late that night when Philip Quest let himself into his office with his key and entered the consulting-room. Lester was sitting up for him, and handed him a bulky letter bearing the Oxford post mark, as the detective sank wearily into a chair.

Quest ripped open the envelope and slowly read the contents, and as he read the reason why Deering had wished for the box to be delivered to Sir Lionel was revealed.

The letter was an answer to the one Quest had sent to his agent in Oxford and it proved beyond a shadow of doubt that 'Snowy' Deering, the man who died in the Lambeth garret, uncared for and unmourned, had been Sir Lionel Trevor's own son!

13

Gathering the Threads

The following day was a busy one, and Philip Quest was astir early, for when Richard Lester came down to breakfast he found that his partner had already gone out.

There was a note beside his plate, however, and Lester opened it as he sat down to attack the appetising dish of bacon and eggs which was set before him. The note was brief and read:

'Take the photograph of Benson which you will find in my desk and go round to all safe deposits and banks in the City. Enquire if they can recognise the photograph as one of their customers. In all probability you will find that if they do they will not recognise it under the name of Benson, but some other name.

'Report here immediately you are successful.

Lester considered this as he ate his breakfast. After all it was rather a tall order. As far as the safe deposits were concerned there were not many, but the banks ... Lester whistled softly as he visualised the number of banks that it would be necessary for him to call on, and almost choked himself with a piece of toast doing so. However, he had asked Quest to give him something to do, and it was better than remaining at home kicking his heels doing nothing.

After breakfast he set off citywards on his mission. The morning was bright and clear, a fact for which he was thankful, for nothing is worse than the City of London on a wet day.

He decided to begin his investigations among the safe deposits, and started with Lombard Street, but here he drew a blank. From building to building he made his way, but in every case his enquiries were attended with the same result. No one could recognise the photograph which he tendered as bearing the slightest resemblance to any of their customers.

By lunch time he had called on them all with the exception of the safe deposit in Chancery Lane, and Lester decided to try this before starting on his round of the banks.

He was courteously received by the manager, a rather stoutish man with a bald head, who listened attentively while Lester briefly stated who he was and the object of his business, and when he had finished the manager took the photograph and carefully examined it.

After a little while he nodded his head slowly.

'Yes, I think I can help you,' he said. 'I am not sure, but I seem to recognise this as the photograph of a man who rented one of our safes about two months ago. I am not quite certain, but I will call the clerk who attended to him at that time.'

He rang a bell on his desk and a page entered.

'Ask Mr. Gregg to come here for a

moment,' said the manager and the boy withdrew.

In a little while a young man with an alert face and sharp, keen eyes entered the office. He glanced enquiringly at the manager.

'Come here a moment, Gregg,' said that gentleman, beckoning him over to the desk. 'Do you remember this man renting a safe from us a short time ago?'

He handed the photograph of Benson to the clerk.

Gregg glanced at it and nodded at once.

'Yes, sir,' he replied. 'He rented safe twenty-five and paid for it six months in advance. The next day he came in and deposited a small deed box. He hasn't been in since.'

'What name did he rent it under?' asked Lester.

'I think the name was Fryer,' replied the clerk after a moment's thought. 'I am not quite certain, but I will make sure. I won't keep you a moment.'

He left the office but returned almost immediately, bearing under his arm a large ledger. Laying it on the desk he rapidly turned the pages, while Lester and the manager bent over him.

Presently he stopped and ran his finger down a page that was filled with names beginning with F.

'Yes, here you are,' he said. 'Charles Fryer, 290, Broad Lane Gardens, Finchley. Safe twenty-five.' Pointing to the entry.

Lester's heart gave a little bound as he read the address, for he knew that he had succeeded in his mission sooner than he had expected. There was no possible doubt that Charles Fryer and Charles Benson had been one and the same person, for Benson's private address had also been 290, Broad Lane Gardens, Finchley.

He thanked the manager for his trouble, took his departure and hurried back to the office. His enquiries at the other places had taken some time, and it was well after lunch when he arrived there. He found Philip Quest in the consulting-room engaged in examining a mass of papers and documents which littered the desk in front of him.

'Well, what luck?' asked the detective as he entered.

'I've discovered what you wanted to know,' cried Lester excitedly. 'Benson rented a safe at the Chancery Lane safe deposit about two months ago, in the name of Charles Fryer, and deposited a deed box there the day after. Since then he hasn't been near the place.'

Quest's eyes gleamed as he heard the news.

'Good!' he cried, patting his partner on the shoulder. 'You've done splendidly. It was a long shot, and I must say I scarcely dared hope that it would come off, but it has, and with any luck we should have the final link necessary to convict the 'Stranger' in our hands within an hour.'

'What is it you expect to find in the safe?' asked Lester.

'The box, Lester,' replied Quest. 'The mysterious box that the 'Stranger' has been searching for all this time, and which was stolen from Audrey Nesbitt's flat by Charles Benson, and which, incidentally, was the reason why he was killed.'

Richard Lester opened his eyes in astonishment.

'Of course! What a fool I am,' he exclaimed. 'That must be the deed box that he deposited in the safe. But how in the world did you know it would be in a safe deposit?'

Quest chuckled.

'I didn't,' he confessed. 'But I thought it was quite possible, and took a chance; as it happens I was lucky.' He rose to his feet. 'I am going out now,' he said as he crossed to the door. 'If Johnson calls keep him here till I come back. I should be home again about six.'

'Where are you going now?' asked his partner.

'I am going to collect that box,' said Quest, 'before it has a chance of disappearing again.'

But he didn't go direct to Chancery Lane. First of all he drove to a firm of solicitors in Bedford Row, and for a long time he was closeted with the senior partner, a Mr. Monkton, who listened with interest to that which the detective had to tell him. When Philip Quest finally set off for Chancery Lane the solicitor accompanied him.

They were some time at the safe deposit, but when they emerged Quest was carrying in his hand a small black box. From Chancery Lane they took a cab and returned to the solicitor's private office, and with the door locked the box was opened. For over two hours they made a close examination of the papers it contained, and at the end of that time Quest had learned the full story of the 'Devil's Dozen.'

'Most extraordinary,' remarked the solicitor when they had completed their examination. 'Most extraordinary. There is no doubt that Deering was Sir Lionel's son. This letter and the papers provide irrefutable proof.'

He handed a single sheet of paper across to the detective and Quest read:

'MY DEAR FATHER,
'By the time you receive this I shall be in my grave.

'I have been a waster all my life and the fault has been all my own.

'There is a streak of pride, however, that runs through all our veins which has prevented me from flaunting this fact to the world in my own name.

'I enclose with this letter the few remaining papers I have left which serve to link me with the past, and also a document which I trust you will place in the hands of the police in the event of anything happening to me.

'We quarrelled once, bitterly. I admit now, though too late, that the fault was mine. Good-bye.

'Your Son,
'ROBERT TREVOR.'

Quest handed the letter back to Monkton in silence. The last words of that poor, drug-wrecked piece of flotsam, who might have ended so differently, had affected him deeply.

'He was evidently ashamed to let his father know that he had sunk so low,' said the solicitor, as he folded the letter. 'That must have been the reason he didn't wish

216

the proofs of his identity contained in this box to reach Sir Lionel until after he himself was dead. I remember the circumstances of the quarrel well, and had often spoken to Sir Lionel about it, in fact I did all in my power to try and effect a reconciliation between them, but Sir Lionel was a hard man, and he considered that it was his son's duty to make the first move towards patching up the quarrel. Of course we had no idea where he was or even that he was alive.'

'With regard to the other document,' said Quest, 'I think that with it in our possession we have sufficient evidence to lay before the Home Secretary.'

'Oh, quite,' agreed the solicitor.

'Then perhaps you wouldn't object,' continued Quest, 'to coming round with me and supporting my story.'

'Not in the least,' declared the solicitor. 'I shall only be too pleased to do anything I can in the matter.'

'I must ask you,' said Quest, as Monkton rose, 'not to mention to a soul the facts contained in Deering's statement at the moment. Particularly the real name of the 'Stranger'.'

'You can rely on me absolutely,' replied Monkton, and they set off for the Home Secretary's office.

They arrived to find that he had already gone home, and they had to go to his private residence. He had just sat down to his dinner, and was not at all pleased at being disturbed, but after Quest had assured him of the urgency of the visit he at least listened attentively to the detective's story.

'I must admit that it is a very strange tale you have told me, Mr. Quest, and I quite agree with you,' he said when Quest had come to the end of the narrative. 'It is most certainly a case for a reprieve. I will attend to the matter at once, and if you will call round some time to-morrow, I will have the document ready to be countersigned by His Majesty!'

Quest thanked him and he and Mr. Monkton took their departure. Outside the house Quest paused and shook hands with the solicitor.

'I am greatly indebted to you for the trouble you have taken,' he said, 'and I should like to ask you one more favour. I should be glad, Mr. Monkton, if you would take charge of the box until to-morrow night. I feel that it will be safer in your hands.'

The solicitor assented readily, and bidding Quest good-bye hailed a taxi and drove rapidly away, and Philip Quest made his way in the direction of the City.

Lester was reading by the fire when he entered his consulting-room.

'Hello!' he cried. 'Did you get the box?'

'I did,' replied the detective, crossing to his desk. 'Has Johnson been round?'

Lester shook his head.

'No, no one's been,' he answered. 'The afternoon has been about as exciting as a flower show in a fog.'

Quest was silent for a moment, then he chuckled softly and drew the telephone towards him.

'What are you laughing at?' demanded his partner.

'What I imagine Johnson will look like when I give my message,' smiled Quest.

He gave a number and in a few minutes was through to Scotland Yard and was talking to Detective-Inspector Johnson.

'Hello, Johnson,' said Quest. 'What are you doing to-morrow evening at eight?'

'To-morrow evening,' repeated the gruff voice of the Inspector. 'Nothing that I know of. Why?'

'I'm giving a little dinner at my flat,' said Quest, 'and I thought you might like to come. Just a few friends, that's all.'

'Look here, Quest,' spluttered Johnson's voice over the wire, 'are you pulling my leg? What the deuce are you giving a dinner for?'

'So that you can meet the 'Stranger',' replied Quest, and hung up the receiver with a chuckle, leaving Inspector Johnson at the other end on the verge of an apoplectic stroke!

14

The Story of the Devil's Dozen

The hands of the little clock that stood on the mantelpiece in Philip Quest's consulting-room pointed to five minutes to eight.

Outside it was raining heavily, and the wet street looked cold and uninviting.

Lester, who had been standing by the window, turned with a grunt of disgust and crossed over to the cheery fire. He was considerably annoyed, an annoyance that was based on the fact that he considered that he had a grievance. Philip Quest had gone out early that morning leaving his partner kicking his heels with nothing to do, and he had remained absent all day, and Lester's grievance was due to the fact that he had not the slightest idea where his partner had gone or what he was doing.

He heard Quest promise Inspector Johnson

to introduce him to the 'Stranger' that evening, and the time was now nearly eight o'clock, and up to the present nothing had happened. Nor was there any message or sign from the detective.

So he considered that he had good reason to grumble at thus being kept in the dark. It had been wet, too, all day and he had not been able to go out, and altogether he felt thoroughly bored and fed up.

At two minutes to eight there came the sound of a key in the lock of the front door, followed by the noise of a step on the stairs, and shortly after the consulting-room door opened and Quest entered. He looked tired and haggard but there was a sparkle in the depths of his keen grey eyes, a triumphant gleam that showed Lester that all was going well.

'No one arrived yet?' he enquired as he crossed to the fire and warmed his hands at the blaze.

'No,' replied Lester in surprise. 'Who were you expecting?'

The detective looked up and surveyed

his young partner with the suspicion of a smile twisting the corners of his lips.

'I sent a note to every one concerned in the case,' he said, 'to meet me here at eight o'clock to-night. Apparently at the moment — ' He broke off. 'That sounds like Johnson now,' he added, and Lester heard the gruff voice of the Inspector from below as he made some remark to the maid in the hall.

A few seconds later the door opened, the maid announced him, and the burly Scotland Yard man entered the room.

'Hope I'm not late, Quest,' he jerked, as he advanced and shook the detective's hand.

'You're the first arrival, Johnson,' smiled Quest, waving him into a chair and pushing forward a box of cigars.

The Inspector took one and lit it with evident satisfaction.

'Well, Quest,' he said with a grin. 'I'm looking forward to meeting the 'Stranger'.'

'I don't think you're going to be disappointed,' answered the detective.

He crossed to his desk and, opening a drawer, took out an automatic, which he examined with care, and, to the astonishment of Lester, slipped into his pocket.

'What time do you expect him?' asked Johnson facetiously, puffing contentedly at his cigar.

'Any time between now and ten o'clock,' replied Quest gravely, and the Inspector was so surprised that he simply stared at the detective with his mouth open, unable to find a suitable reply.

'Here!' ejaculated Lester, his eyes round with amazement.

'Certainly,' said Quest smiling. 'I have invited a few friends to meet him.'

'But,' exploded the young man, 'how do you know he will come! Why should he?'

'Because I asked him,' replied the detective quietly, and Lester made a gesture of despair.

'I wish you wouldn't talk in riddles, and anyway, I don't see why you should be so jolly close about it, and keep a chap in the dark.'

'Oh, let him have his way,' grunted Johnson. 'He likes these little theatrical surprise packets, they amuse him.'

'But — ' began Lester, when Quest stopped him.

'I think I can hear some of our guests arriving,' he said, and he had scarcely finished speaking when Audrey Nesbitt, accompanied by Jack Archer, came in.

They had hardly exchanged greetings with their host and Inspector Johnson and Lester before they were followed by Norman Carfax and a stranger, a medium-sized, bearded man, with a florid complexion. He carried a small bag in his hand which he set down carefully on a side table before shaking hands with Quest. The detective took him to one side and said something to him in a low voice. Then he turned to the others.

'I expect you are all aware from my note,' said Quest, when they were all seated, 'of the object of my asking you to meet me here this evening.'

He glanced round and received affirmative nods.

'It is my intention,' he continued, seating himself in a chair which enabled him to face everyone present, 'to clear up to-night the mystery surrounding the organisation known as the 'Devil's Dozen,' to reveal the real murderer of Charles Benson, the reason for the killing of Sir Lionel Trevor, and' — he paused — 'to unmask the identity of the most dangerous and elusive criminal of modern times — the 'Stranger'!'

He looked at the expectant faces before him. Audrey Nesbitt was as pale as death, her hands played nervously, twisting and untwisting themselves in her lap. Jack Archer appeared to be unconcerned, but the effort it cost him was revealed in the whiteness of his knuckles as his hands gripped the arms of his chair. Norman Carfax was leaning forward in his seat gazing at Philip Quest, an expression of interest on his good-looking face. The bearded stranger was looking fixedly at the window, his eyes expressionless, and presenting the picture of utter indifference and intense boredom with the whole proceedings.

'As all of us have been closely concerned with the case,' Quest went on, 'I thought it would be of interest for you to be present at its final stages.'

'Do you mean, Quest,' asked Carfax, 'that you know the identity of the 'Stranger'?'

Quest nodded.

'I do,' he said simply. 'I have known his identity for the past three days.'

'And you haven't arrested him?' cried Carfax, incredulously.

'I have not,' answered the detective quietly, 'the time was not right. I expect to arrest him — to-night!'

'To-night! Where?' asked Jack Archer.

'Here!' said Quest.

'Here!' echoed Carfax in astonishment. 'Do you expect him here?'

'Before ten o'clock,' said Quest deliberately, 'the 'Stranger' will be in this room!'

A silence followed his words. The atmosphere of the room had of a sudden grown strangely tense, a tenseness not unlike that which usually precedes a thunderstorm. Philip Quest settled himself more comfortably in his chair, and clearing his throat, began again.

'In order that you will be able to follow easily what I am about to tell you,' he commenced, 'I will recapitulate as briefly as possible a few facts which are known to some of you present but not, I think, to all.

'About twelve months ago there suddenly sprang into being an organisation which became known as the 'Devil's Dozen.' The man responsible for its inception was an unknown and mysterious individual, who, worked under the pseudonym of the 'Stranger.'

'His *modus operandi* was to find somebody who was either in need of money or was in fear of prosecution for some offence against the law which he or she had committed. He took the utmost precaution and made the most careful enquiries before approaching each recruit. In this way, in a surprisingly short time, he collected around him a number of assistants, eleven in all, each one of whom was unknown to the others, but all known to the 'Stranger.' His real identity, of course, was a mystery to all of them.

'The idea, you will admit, was a clever one, for under no circumstances could any one member of the gang give the others away — or their mysterious and elusive leader.

'It had one disadvantage from their point of view for it put them completely at the mercy of the 'Stranger.' I believe he had some such idea in his mind when the gang was first formed, anyhow, whether he did or not, he quickly took advantage of it after.'

Quest paused again for a moment.

'Having used the gang to further his own ends the 'Stranger' conceived the idea of retaining all the proceeds from their various and far-reaching activities, for himself. Possibly it had been in his mind from the start — we can't say — but with this end in view he put into practice a dastardly scheme.'

Quest stopped again for a moment and looked at his listeners, then went on:

'There is an old saying about 'there being honour amongst thieves,' but in this particular case there was nothing that could be further from the truth.

'His scheme, in a nut shell, was to give away his associates to the police, so that they could be caught red-handed in the act of committing a crime that he had himself planned, and by that means get rid of them one by one. It was a devilish idea and worthy of the man who thought of it!

'The first case in which the 'Stranger' tried this plan was the Benson murder. It was he who killed Charles Benson and he had a double motive for doing so.

'Among the members of the gang was a young man named Deering — it was not his real name, but that is by the way — he was a man of good family and education, but had ruined himself by drugs. Deering soon became suspicious of the 'Stranger,' and discovered the plans he had made for double-crossing the others. During his enquiries he found out the real identity of the mysterious leader of the gang. He knew that if the 'Stranger' became aware of this his life would not be worth a moment's purchase and to safe-guard himself, set down the result of his discoveries in writing which he placed, together with some other papers, in a box and posted it to Miss Nesbitt, with a covering note asking if she would, in event of his death, deliver the box immediately into the hands of Sir Lionel

Trevor, her employer.

'Charles Benson, although posing as a prosperous City merchant was in reality one of the first to be recruited to the 'Stranger' gang. Deering met him during the time he was making his enquiries concerning the 'Stranger,' and became aware that he was a fellow member.

'This, I believe, was the only time, until recently, that any two members of the 'Devil's Dozen' became aware of each other's identity. They met several times after, and on one occasion Benson came to see Deering at Lambeth.

'Deering, up to a point, confided in Benson. He did not tell him all he knew, but enough for Benson to learn about the box and its contents, and to whom it had been sent.

'Benson at this time was getting rather fed up with acting under the 'Stranger's' orders, particularly as he had received very little in return, and he saw in what 'Snowy' Deering had told him a chance to quickly clean up a small fortune and sever his connection with the gang for good and all.

'He made up his mind to secure the box, learn from its contents the real identity of the 'Stranger' and blackmail him into giving him a sum that would be sufficient, with what he already had of his own, to keep him in comfort for the rest of his life. He knew that the box, a veritable box of doom as far as the 'Stranger' was concerned, had been sent to a Miss Audrey Nesbitt. He was acquainted with her slightly as she was engaged to his secretary and had once or twice been to his office. He concluded that the box was in her flat, and one night when he had ascertained that she was going to a theatre with Archer he entered the flat by the aid of a skeleton key, and stole the box. On examining the contents he found, as well as the documents that Deering had mentioned, a number of private papers, which, to his surprise, proved that Deering was Sir Lionel Trevor's son!'

Audrey Nesbitt suppressed a little gasp of astonishment at Quest's words.

The detective went on:

'Benson was now in possession of the

information he needed, and he proceeded to put his plan of blackmail into execution.

'In the meanwhile the 'Stranger' had become aware of the existence of the document in which Deering had set down the result of his discoveries, and he knew that it contained an exposure of his real identity, and that while it remained undestroyed it was a constant source of danger to himself. How he found this out I am not quite certain, and as far as we are concerned it matters very little. It is sufficient that I can prove conclusively that he did know of its existence, and it was this knowledge which led, later, to Sir Lionel's death.

'Deering died, and the 'Stranger' was now in a worse position than he had been while Deering lived. At all costs it was necessary for him to find out what had happened to the documents and prevent it falling into anyone's hands who might use it to betray him.

'From Deering's landlady he learned that she had posted for Deering a parcel addressed to Sir Lionel Trevor's house in

Portman Square. This fact, as far as the 'Stranger' was concerned, was significant, for he already knew what Benson discovered from the papers and what I have only recently found out, that Deering was in reality Sir Lionel Trevor's son. He immediately concluded, wrongly as it turned out, that Deering had sent the document to his father, and he determined to seek for it at Sir Lionel's house. But in the meanwhile the 'Stranger' received a letter from Benson which contained a further shock. Benson had started his plan for blackmail and he saw at once another menace to his safety.

'How Benson had discovered his identity he was unaware, but the fact that he knew was sufficient, and he had to be silenced at once. The 'Stranger' agreed to Benson's terms and fixed an appointment to see him at his office to pay over the money, and here the idea came to him to get rid of two members of the gang at the same time. He wrote to Jefferson Harlowe enclosing the keys to Benson's offices, which had been easy enough for him to obtain, and instructed him to go there that evening, on the pretext of robbing the safe.

'He fixed the time for Harlowe's arrival so that it was exactly a quarter of an hour after the time at which he intended to keep his own appointment with Benson.

'Benson had that morning drawn all his money from the bank, and was ready, directly he received the sum expected from the 'Stranger' to leave the country.

'The 'Stranger' kept his appointment and killed him. Opening the safe with Benson's keys he removed the money, placed it in an envelope and threw it out of the window, where it was picked up by a man named Bennet, who was a member of the 'Devil's Dozen,' and had been placed there for that purpose by the 'Stranger'.

'Everything was now prepared for the arrival of Jefferson Harlowe a quarter of an hour later. Only one thing remained to make the 'frame up' complete. The 'Stranger' left Benson's office and made his way at once to the nearest telephone, and from there he sent the message to Scotland Yard stating that the murder had been committed.'

Philip Quest stopped for a moment, and leaning back in his chair, pressed the tips of his long lean fingers together.

'As you know,' he continued, 'his plan succeeded, and Harlowe was arrested, tried, and found guilty of the murder of Benson. The 'Stranger,' however, was still in a panic, for though he had successfully dealt with Benson he had still to find the document prepared by Deering.

'The result of his enquiries at Lambeth led him to suppose that Deering had sent it to his father, and the 'Stranger' decided to leave no stone unturned to gain possession of it. With this end in view he wrote to Sir Lionel a letter demanding the return of the box, and stating a place at which it was to be turned over to him.

'The 'Stranger,' receiving no reply to his letter, decided to break into Portman Square. He was in the act of searching the study when Sir Lionel was awakened by some noise downstairs, and discovered him. The 'Stranger' was wearing a black silk mask and in the brief struggle which ensued Sir Lionel managed to tear this mask from his face, catching a strand of the silk in his finger nail as he did so. As the mask came off Sir Lionel recognised the intruder. The 'Stranger' knew that he had been recognised and that if Sir Lionel lived the game was up, so he shot him with a pistol to which was attached a silencer, and made his escape.

'That is the story of how Benson died and the reason for the killing of Sir Lionel Trevor.'

Quest stopped, glanced at the clock, and leaned forward in his chair, slipping his hands unconcernedly into the side pockets of his jacket.

'I told you, Johnson,' he said, looking over at the Scotland Yard man, 'that to-night I would introduce to you the 'Stranger.' I have succeeded in discovering the box which contains irrefutable proof of his real identity, and Mr. Monkton' — he looked across at the bearded stranger, who was still gazing at the window with a bored expression on his face — 'who was Sir Lionel's solicitor, has it in his possession, and is prepared to hand over the contents to you. I have already read and it proves without a shadow of a doubt the identity of the 'Stranger.'

'I made a statement a short while ago that before ten o'clock the 'Stranger' would be in this room. It is now nine-thirty and — if you move so much as a finger I'll blow the top of your head off!' He snapped the words out like the shot from a gun.

An automatic pistol had appeared as if by magic in his hand, and it was levelled directly at Norman Carfax!

There was a gasp of astonishment from Inspector Johnson and Lester, followed by an instant's silence, which was broken by Carfax.

'Look here,' he began angrily, his face white, 'if this is a joke — '

'It's no joke, Carfax,' cut in the detective sternly. 'The game's up, and you know it. You knew it when you tried to get me the other morning in Oxford Street. I've got enough proof in that box to hang you a dozen times over. You've been very clever, but you made just two little mistakes. I told you once that all criminals make them sooner or later. The first you made when you forgot to remove all the traces of the beard you had been wearing before you called me up in the night your flat was broken into. A slight portion of it still remained adhering to your chin. The second was when you kept your trousers on, and your waistcoat, under your pyjamas on the same occasion. I noticed both points immediately on my arrival and my suspicions of you dated from that time. And another point, taken in conjunction with the other facts, made them almost a certainty.

'You remember the piece of elastic, Johnson, which was in Sir Lionel's study with the blood mark on it? I said at the time that it would help to identify the murderer. The blood came from that small scratch on Carfax's face where Sir Lionel's nail caught in the silk as he ripped the mask off — '

'Look out!' yelled Lester.

Norman Carfax made a sudden quick dive and caught Audrey Nesbitt by the waist, swinging the girl between himself and Philip Quest so that she was directly in the line of the detective's fire. Whipping a pistol from his pocket with his free hand he backed to the door, still keeping the terrified girl in front of him as a shield.

'You haven't got me yet, Quest,' he panted, glaring at the detective, 'but I'll give you something to remember me by.'

There was a deafening explosion and Quest ducked quickly. The bullet missed him and thudded into the wall.

Carfax growled out a curse, and was preparing to fire again when the door behind him was suddenly jerked open and his pistol hand gripped in a grasp of iron. The next instant there was a jangle of steel and Carfax was securely hand-cuffed between two plain clothes men, and Quest caught Audrey Nesbitt as she staggered and almost fell.

'Take him away,' said Quest as he handed the half-fainting girl over to the care of Jack Archer.

'Curse you, Quest, you cunning devil,' snarled Carfax, struggling in the grip of the two policemen as they forced him towards the door. 'If I'd only got you that time in Oxford Street — '

'You did your best, Carfax,' said Quest coolly. 'It was a good idea, but such a damned bad shot!'

★　★　★

'Now perhaps you'll do a little explaining, Quest,' suggested Inspector Johnson, some ten minutes later. 'There are still several points on which I am still in the dark.'

'Hear, hear,' echoed Lester, 'come on partner, spill the beans.'

Carfax had been taken away and they were in the detective's consulting-room. Audrey Nesbitt and Jack Archer had remained, but the solicitor, Mr. Monkton, had departed, after leaving the box in charge of the Scotland Yard man.

'I shall be pleased to answer any questions you may ask,' said Quest with a smile. 'And as I am expecting a friend of mine here at any moment, I suggest you fire away and get it over.'

'Perhaps if you are expecting a visitor,'

said Audrey, 'you would rather we didn't stay.'

'I wish you to stay. In fact I am particularly anxious for you to meet the person I am expecting.'

The girl looked surprised, but she made no remark. She felt too content to wonder much at anything, for the worry of months had been swept away and a vista of complete happiness lay before her.

'Well, to start with, Quest,' began Johnson, 'I want to know how you discovered the whereabouts of that box.'

'It was really very simple, Johnson,' said the detective, 'and purely a matter of reasoning. Whoever had stolen the box from Miss Nesbitt's flat must have been aware of the contents, and it was fairly safe to suppose that the only way he could have learned this was from Deering himself. We knew that the 'Stranger' was aware of what the box contained, but the 'Stranger' could not have stolen it from Miss Nesbitt because he was still looking for it. This clearly meant that it had been taken by a third person. Now, who was the most likely person? The answer was obviously someone who was fairly friendly with Deering, and to whom he had communicated the contents of the box.

'I remembered the landlady at Lambeth mentioning that an elderly man had called to see Deering once, and I obtained from her a description of this visitor. The description she gave fitted Charles Benson, and I made certain by showing her a photograph of the dead man which I obtained from you. She identified it immediately as the same man.

'In this way I was able to connect Deering with Benson, and a point that helped me to arrive at my conclusion that it was Benson who had taken the box was strengthened when I became acquainted with the fact that Jack Archer and Miss Nesbitt were engaged. I ascertained that she often called at Benson's office, and it struck me that in this way he would be able easily to learn when the coast was clear for him to obtain the box. The question now remaining was, what had

Benson, supposing he was the person who had stolen it, done with the box? I confess that here I took a long shot.

'The police had thoroughly examined all his effects at the time of the murder, and if the box had been among them it would have been found then. I spent some time thinking the matter over, and I put myself in Benson's place. The box must have contained some item of valuable information and I had already concluded that it was some kind of papers that in some way implicated the 'Stranger' for he would never have taken the tremendous risks he did to obtain it if that had not been so. Besides which Deering was, at the time it was sent, in abject poverty.

'Taking this as a working hypothesis, I formed the theory that if the contents of the box implicated the 'Stranger' the most natural conclusion to arrive at was that they contained something that was a clue to his real identity. In which case, if Benson had discovered this it was possible that he had attempted blackmail.

'It was only a theory but I worked on it.

I concluded that if I was correct the most likely place for the box to be was somewhere where it was only accessible to Benson himself. The most natural place would have been his bank, but I knew it was not there. The only possible solution was that he had deposited it somewhere in another name.

'I sent Lester, armed with a photograph of Benson, round the most likely places and my long shot was a lucky one. At Chancery Lane safe deposit the photograph was recognised as that of a man who had hired a safe in the name of Fryer. I saw the manager and after I had explained the situation he opened the safe and we found the box. What it contained you already know.'

'How did you know definitely that Benson was trying to blackmail Carfax?' asked Lester.

'I found a copy of the letter he had written among the papers in the box,' answered the detective. 'I also knew he was a member of the 'Devil's Dozen' because Deering had mentioned the fact in his statement.'

'I suppose Carfax faked the burglary at his flat to throw suspicion away from himself?' remarked Johnson.

Philip Quest glanced across at Audrey Nesbitt with a twinkle in his eye.

'He faked the card bearing the signature of the 'Stranger,'' he replied, 'but he wasn't responsible for the burglary. Miss Nesbitt did that, searching for proofs of her father's innocence. Directly Carfax realised who had broken into his flat, and after he had attempted my life in Oxford Street, he went straight to Miss Nesbitt's flat to look for the box which he was now convinced was in her possession. It's very lucky,' he added to the girl, 'that you escaped with your life on that occasion.'

'Who was the grey-bearded man who followed us to the tea shop?' enquired Jack Archer.

'Carfax, of course,' replied Quest. 'It was his favourite disguise, and it was my fault that he was following Miss Nesbitt. When he called to see me just after Sir Lionel's murder, I very foolishly told him that I had discovered the box had been posted to you. Of course, I had no suspicion of him at the time. He must have gone home, donned his disguise, and set off to break into Miss Nesbitt's flat. I imagine that it was the sight of Lester that put him off on that occasion. He followed the three of you, and arranged his plan to get rid of Lester, which he nearly succeeded in doing.

'On arriving home he must have been surprised to find that someone, in his absence, had burgled his own flat. He tried to turn it to his own advantage by phoning me and telling me that it was the work of the 'Devil's Dozen.'

'In regard to the Benson murder, I learned most of the details from the man Bennet. Carfax, in his disguise of the 'Stranger,' told Bennet that Benson and Harlowe were traitors to the gang, and were double-crossing them. He tried to work the same trick on Bennet and Grogan as he did on Harlowe. Having instructed them that Lester was to be killed, he immediately phoned to the police at Horsham giving them away, hoping that they would be caught red-handed, and if it hadn't been for Archer, his scheme would probably have been successful.'

'What a diabolical scoundrel!' exclaimed Jack Archer, 'and yet you'd never think it was possible to look at him.'

'That was his greatest asset in the double life he led,' said Philip Quest. 'He was very popular in his own capacity of Norman Carfax, K.C., and quite a good barrister too.'

'The suit-cases at the various stations was an ingenious idea,' commented Johnson. 'At any hour he was prepared for a quick get-away. I congratulate you, Quest, on the way you've worked it all out.'

'But what about the rest of the gang?' asked Lester. 'There were always supposed to be twelve, weren't there?'

'There were twelve,' answered Quest, 'including Carfax. We've got six; as far as the other six are concerned I don't think we need worry much about them. Without their leader they aren't likely to be very dangerous.'

'Well, Quest,' said Johnson, rising to his

feet, 'I think I'll be off. I must say' — his eyes twinkled — 'that I've enjoyed your little party immensely.'

He shook hands with the detective and said good-bye to the others, and, carrying the box which had been the cause of so much excitement in his hand, took his departure.

He had scarcely gone before there came a ring at the front door bell.

'Excuse me,' Philip Quest murmured, and slipped out of the room.

'I suppose there is nothing now to prevent father being released,' said Audrey in a low voice. 'Oh, I'm so glad it's all over and that we shall be able to live normally again without — '

She broke off and stared at the door.

Philip Quest had returned and with him entered a tall, soldierly-looking man, with silver grey hair and moustache.

'Miss Nesbitt,' smiled the detective, 'let me introduce you to the friend I was expecting — Mr. Jefferson Harlowe!'

'Father!'

'Audrey!'

The two voices rang out together and

the next instant the girl was clasped in her father's arms and lay sobbing gently, while he pressed his cheek to her fair hair.

'Come, Lester,' said Quest softly as he touched his partner on the arm. 'This is no place for a stranger.'

'No, the place, for a 'Stranger' is in Wandsworth Prison,' murmured Lester with a chuckle as he followed the detective quietly from the room.

THE END